DELUSIONS

JOELLE STEELE

Many Hats Publications
A Division Of
Jöelle Steele Enterprises

This novel is a work of fiction. Any references to people, places, or events are solely the product of the author's imagination or are used in a fictional way to enhance the story.

ISBN: 978-1-940388-23-6 (print book)
ISBN: 978-1-940388-22-9 (ebook)

Jöelle Steele Enterprises/Many Hats Publications
United States of America
www.manyhatspublications.com

Printed in the United States of America

ACKNOWLEDGMENTS

Thanks to Gretchen Wilding and Liz Hart-Graham for their content editing and research talents; to Melanie Zwick and Ronald Morrissey for their knowledge of schizophrenia and their experience with the social services system in California; to Fr. Donald L. Rice and Michael W. Cuneo for their knowledge of exorcism and the Roman Catholic Church; and to Diever Bluhm for his expertise in the field of geotechnical engineering.

The boundaries which divide Life from Death are at best shadowy and vague.

Edgar Allan Poe
The Premature Burial, 1844

Knowing that you're crazy doesn't make the crazy things stop happening.

Mark Vonnegut
The Eden Express: A Memoir of Insanity

Maybe all the people who say ghosts don't exist are just afraid to admit that they do.

Michael Ende
The Neverending Story

I no longer knew what was real and what wasn't. The lines between reality and delusion had become so blurred.

A.B. Shepherd
The Beacon

DELUSIONS

In the abyss of superstition
lives amiss an apparition,
remnants of my sad delusions.

Everyday hallucination
fired by my imagination
masquerades beside me like a ghost.

It can't see that I'm demented,
wed to thoughts so quick-cemented
to the very fabric of my soul.

Amid the mists of the allusion
to my wax-and-wane confusion
answers waft along as plain as day.

What I perceive, I can believe.
A glimpse from my cursed eyes
says what I see, and all I see, is truth.

Or not.

CHAPTER 1

Amanda Woods twisted the rod that closed the mini-blinds. That was better. Now she could see the TV without the glare of the afternoon sun hitting the screen and, as an extra benefit, the Benzos couldn't spy on her for a while. It was almost time for *A Time For Love* to start and she plopped down on the sofa, releasing an explosion of dust. She should vacuum again someday.

She unpeeled and ate a banana while a string of boring commercials blared. She rolled her eyes in frustration as one after another drug commercials rolled by. She wanted to watch her show. She was anxious to see what her best friend, nurse Grace Peterson, was up to in the town of Maple Valley in upstate New York, where Valley Medical Center was located. They had spoken on the phone earlier that morning, and Grace told her that Jack Benson was a good guy, even though Amanda saw him kissing pediatrician Molly Harrison as she struggled to get away from him. And after having brain surgery, Jack was supposed to be normal and a much nicer person! She hoped Grace wasn't falling for that, but then Grace was always so forgiving, so understanding, so ...

"Mandy! Mandy!" It was her mother. Rhoda Pruitt's timing was impeccable as usual. The woman had a knack for creating a disturbance whenever Amanda was trying to have a moment to herself, a moment when things were relatively quiet in the world.

"Go away, Rhoda," she yelled towards the stairs leading to her mother's bedroom. She never called her Mom or Mother. She hardly knew the woman.

"Mandy! You can't ignore me!"

She hated it when Rhoda called her Mandy. She wasn't a child anymore. She was an adult and had preferred to be called Amanda since she was 15. Her mother knew that, even though she didn't see Amanda after the age of 5. So why did she keep calling her Mandy? Why? Why? Why?

"Mandy! Get in here this minute!"

She also hated to go into Rhoda's bedroom and avoided it whenever possible. It was a mess amid the clutter of a terminal illness, like a hoarder's warehouse for things that weren't necessary but were obsessively collected 'just in case.' There was a mountain range of towels, blankets, and dirty laundry that surrounded the four-poster mahogany bed that dwarfed her mother's small frame. And as if that were not enough, the ceilings were dotted with cobwebs inhabited by dangling, long-legged spiders. She had twice found black widows living under the edges of the bookcases near the baseboards. There were probably brown recluse spiders in there too ... somewhere. She didn't want to think about it. And, like the rest of the house, the room reeked of ammonia and other chemical smells.

"The Benzos are at it again! Close the windows!"

Rhoda had never been polite in her life, never a sincere please or thank you. And she had become even worse, more unappreciative of her daughter, her only child. Her show was starting and Amanda turned up the TV in an attempt to hear it and simultaneously drown out the nagging voice from upstairs.

Cancer had taken its toll on her mother, and as far as Amanda was concerned, the old woman deserved every minute of suffering she had to endure until the deviant disease made its final attack on the last remaining healthy cells in her bloated, yellowing body. It wouldn't be long now. But she always said that, and yet Rhoda continued to linger.

Only a few minutes into her show and another commercial came on. Amanda ran to the bathroom. She quickly washed the sticky banana residue from her hands and looked at herself in the mirror as she stood in front of the sink. Her complexion was clear and radiant. She never wore make-up. Her long dark lashes framed her deep turquoise eyes, and her face was framed with a mane of thick, dark, wavy hair. She didn't know why that busybody social worker, Linda Cicero, was always nagging her about her appearance. Perhaps she should run a brush through her hair more often, and regular bathing, uninterrupted by Rhoda, was a luxury she wished was a possibility but it wasn't in the cards. Fortunately, her cousin Kimberly understood. She always said, 'Don't worry, Amanda, nobody ever died from being dirty.'

And experts like Linda Cicero thought she was delusional. They didn't even see her for who she was beneath her physical appearance. And at least she knew the meaning of the word 'delusion.' That was a hell of a lot more than they did.

"Delusion," she said out loud and emphatically to only herself, just as a reminder: "An idiosyncratic impression or persistent false psychotic belief regarding the self or persons or objects outside the self that is accepted and maintained as reality or rational despite indisputable evidence to the contrary." She had memorized the definition from a book on schizophrenia she read when she was first diagnosed. She had written it down and given it to Linda Cicero.

She took a last-minute look at herself in the mirror. No one had ever said Amanda looked anything other than drop-dead gorgeous. She was in the prime of her life at 35. No, that wasn't right. It couldn't be 35, could it? Was she that old? Wait, no, maybe it was the other way around. Maybe 35 was too young? Maybe she was 45? That sounded so old. She wished she could remember how old she was. But, it probably didn't matter. She could be 50 and still be a knockout. What did Linda Cicero know anyway?

Linda Cicero was a meddling old fool, always sticking her nose where it didn't belong. She stopped by occasionally, usually on a Wednesday, and usually just in time to disturb Amanda while she was trying to see what was happening in Maple Valley. She had never been to Maple Valley but they broadcast the activities of its residents who worked at the city's Valley Medical Center, and Amanda had known many of them for most of her life. They were friends of her Aunt Margot's in the beginning, but over the years they had become friends of Amanda's. And Linda was trying to keep her from her friends. She even had the nerve to say they weren't really Amanda's friends. What did that do-gooder know anyway? She should stick to taking care of Rhoda and leave Amanda the hell alone.

A simultaneous wave of confusion and nausea came over Amanda as she headed back to the living room. She stood still for a moment, waiting to see if it would pass, and when did she returned to the sitting area in the small living room.

"You're sick too, Mandy, you know that don't you?" called her mother's harsh and accusing voice, executed with an added sing-song lilt.

"Yeah, well, you would know a thing or two about being sick, wouldn't you," she retorted under her breath as she laid back on the couch to watch her show.

When would all of this end? She wanted to be able to watch the handful of TV shows she liked and then sit back and read a book. How much longer was Rhoda going to continue?

"Mandy!"

She cranked up the volume again. There were days when she wished she could burn down the house with Rhoda in it. But she knew that wasn't possible, and it wouldn't help if she did.

CHAPTER 2

St. Lucius Church was in a rural community east of Philadelphia, about halfway to Harrisburg and roughly 34 miles from his parents' home, and 30-year-old Father Elias Antonelli was an enthusiastic and devout priest who was grateful to be posted in the same state, let alone the same general area amidst such familiar surroundings. St. Lucius was originally a small limestone structure built in 1771 by Quakers. But when it was acquired by the Catholic Church in 1886 it was named St. Lucius. The original building was remodeled to serve as the rectory when the new brownstone church was built in 1919.

It was on March 1st, only three days before the Feast Day of St. Lucius, that Father Elias first saw the beautiful old buildings. They made him feel a sense of belonging to something much older and much greater than himself. It wasn't exactly the Vatican, but then, what was? It was certainly far more than he expected for a first posting.

Elias looked like his humble, second-generation Italian roots. He was 5'9" with a wiry build, a light olive complexion, gray eyes, and hair that was dark brown, almost black. He grew up in a small brick walk-up in South Philly, two blocks from the 9th Street grocery store where his father, Pete, was the owner. His mother, Rosa, was a housewife who raised five kids and always found time to participate in a variety of community and church activities. It was the devout, Roman Catholic Rosa who had the strongest influence on Elias, her youngest. It was probably because he was so much like her. While she had to drag his siblings to church and practically beg them to say their prayers at night, Elias was a willing student of God, the Bible, and the Roman Catholic church. Rosa was overjoyed when he announced his intentions to become a priest.

"My boy Elias has decided to become a priest!" she gushed with pride. "Can you imagine? A priest in the family!" She beamed with joy and her smile lit up the room.

"Are you sure this is what you want?" frowned his father, not feeling the same exuberance that his wife did on hearing of his 17-year-old son's weighty life decision.

"I've thought about it long and hard. I am absolutely positive. I have no doubts," he insured his concerned father. "Don't worry about me, Dad. I've known this was the right path for a very long time."

Elias had first heard God calling him when he was 12 years old, and the call became louder with each successive year. He vividly remembered the day when he first felt the pull of the church. It was Saturday, July 17, 1982, and he was profoundly sad at the time. It was almost two weeks after his beloved Nonno's funeral, and the family had arrived at the cabin they rented each year in the Poconos. Elias was old enough to realize that life went on after someone passed away, but he had never expected that his family would still go on their yearly vacation after such a huge loss.

"Nonno would want us to be happy and not dwell on his loss," explained his mother, grieving over the loss of her father.

"But a vacation? Come on, Mom! Shouldn't we at least show respect for Nonno by observing some quiet time, maybe doing our daily life stuff instead?" asked Elias.

"This cabin was his favorite place. We can remember him here and we can just as easily live our daily lives here," she said.

And so Elias came to wander along the banks of Pocono Creek. His frustration caused him to kick at the dirt and branches that lined the rough and seldom-traveled rustic trail. Eventually, he came to a small cataract in the stream where the water cascaded over dark boulders clogged with broken logs and an assortment of other forest debris, eventually flowing into a silent and restful weir before it continued on its journey. He sat down on a log and skipped pebbles and small, flat stones across the almost still water.

And he prayed. And as with all prayer, it was an intimate conversation between him and God, although at times it seemed like too much of a one-way communication. But he believed God knew his heart, and so he was never deterred from the practice. He knew a great many prayers from memory, and he paraphrased the one he had heard at the funeral.

"Dear Lord, please have compassion and mercy for the soul of my grandfather, Mario Cobella. He was a kind and loving man, and he was always good to me. Please, God, forgive him his sins and let me someday meet him again in your great Heaven. Amen."

He sat in silence for awhile and thought about some of the good times he'd had with Nonno. In particular he remembered the many times they went fishing, and all the hours they spent working together in his basement making buildings out of tongue depressors and old popsicle sticks for Nonno' model railroad layout. And then there were all the baseball games. He and Nonno loved going to see the Phillies play, and it wasn't just for the hot dogs! He would never forget the 1980 National League Championship Series they went to when Greg Luzinski hit a game-winning two-run homer. At the time, it was the greatest year to date in the history of the Phillies.

He wished he didn't feel so gloomy and depressed, and he wished that he knew a prayer for overcoming grief. But he didn't, and so he again crafted his own prayer and hoped – knew – that God would hear it.

"Oh, dear God, please lift this awful pain from my heart. I feel so alone, and I know you can help end this grief. Please help me accept the loss of Nonno and move on in my life to do something that will make him proud of me. Amen."

Elias sat staring at the water and watched the clouds reflected in its glassy surface. Nature was truly a miracle. He could feel peace and serenity despite his deep sorrow. And he felt a lifting of his spirit, a realization that he had a place in this world. And he wondered what that place might be, and he again prayed.

"Dear Lord, please show me the way."

That was what Nonno had always said a person should ask of God, because God always knew what was right for each of us at all times throughout our lives.

"Please guide me in the path you have chosen for me in this world. I know I'm still very young, but please help me become the best man I can be. Amen."

And as he took a final look around the little patch of nature he had been enjoying, he had a vision of what he was meant to do in his life. There was no thundering voice echoing throughout the wilderness of the Poconos calling to Elias Antonelli. He simply knew. In his mind's eye, he could see himself as a priest, doing God's work as a spiritual caretaker, ministering to the needs of the faithful.

From that day on, everything Elias thought and did revolved around achieving his goal of becoming a priest. Did he struggle along the way? Of course, and he was still struggling at times. He struggled at first with celibacy. When he was a teenager he thought that would be a hurdle he could never overcome, but he did. It was not as easy to overcome the hurdle of obedience to the Word of God. That was a much greater obstacle. But he persevered, even when he could sometimes not see the right of it. He simply prayed all the harder for God to enlighten him, to continue to show him the way. And maybe that was enough.

Maybe it was more than he had a right to ask. After all, there were a great many mysteries in the Bible, and perhaps mere mortals were not always meant to know and understand their true nature.

After he graduated from high school, Elias went to the University of Pennsylvania in Philadelphia and graduated with a bachelor's degree in Philosophy. After bumming around the world for two years – a time period he felt was an invaluable part of any young person's education, and one that he felt was an indispensible part of his own understanding of the world – he attended St. Charles Borromeo Seminary on the outskirts of Philadelphia and obtained a Master of Divinity.

After his ordination, he came directly to St. Lucius, where he began living the life he knew he was destined to live. Mostly it was a joyful existence, celebrating the mass and all the important spiritual milestones in the lives of the parishioners. But there were also the heartbreaking times, when he presided at a funeral or counseled a troubled individual or family in a time of great need – not always a spiritual one. And then there were those days when he was teaching young children about God and the church, or participating in community activities such as stocking local food pantries, making sandwiches at the soup kitchen, or performing other helping activities. Sometimes it was just plain fun, like playing baseball with the neighborhood kids or attending a soccer game at the nearby Catholic School. Much of his time was spent in prayer and meditation, as he continued to build his relationship with God. And studying. In addition to the Bible, he loved to study and learn new things, and so his evenings were often consumed with reading or watching documentaries on TV. He had regular domestic chores to do too, like cooking, cleaning, laundry, and grocery shopping. And whenever possible, he tried to take some time off to visit with his family.

But whatever he was doing, every minute of every day, Elias devoted himself to God. He never wavered in his faith in the Lord. He believed in God with every beat of his heart – despite his occasional insecurities about blind obedience to the church and his belief in the unseen and unknown. He believed in things outside of God and the Catholic Church, even as he harbored an unanswered plethora of questions about so many of those beliefs.

His difficulty in practicing obedience to the Word of God was made so much worse by his almost obsessive need to tune into the numerous shows about ghosts, hauntings, reinterpretations of history, and alien intervention and its impact on ancient cultures. These activities weren't forbidden. It wasn't a sin to watch them. And Elias was so incredibly curious. And yes, some of those shows were obviously staged and harbored theories that were largely absurd. And yes, some of them had hosts who were undeniably as crazy as the proverbial bedbug. But then again, some of what he heard and saw seemed entirely plausible. Those were the shows that made him think, drove him to read books on these often highly speculative subjects, and made him question everything he thought he knew. And a lot of what he thought he knew was what he learned when he studied for the priesthood.

Fortunately, Elias was now working with an older priest who, at least in part, shared his interest in the more controversial aspects of the spiritual world. During his three years at St. Lucius, he exchanged thoughts and theories with Father Christopher Ignatius, a 72-year-old scholarly man who had weathered many storms and often tiptoed on the edge of controversial practices that the church nevertheless felt were acceptable, including exorcism.

Elias was as fascinated by the idea of demons and demonic possession as he was with the existence of angels. However, he didn't know as much about demons as he did about angels. He believed in angels, and he'd had some academic study of them, while demonology was only one of many things he still planned to study in depth one day. The study of either angels or demons was classified as controversial in his own mind. And there was a part of him that put up a fairly substantial and sturdy barrier when it came to facing the potential dangers that lurked on the 'dark side.'

But, with the study of angels, he had made some steady progress. The very origins of angels, combined with theories of aliens/extraterrestrials visiting ancient cultures, was more than enough to keep him questioning and seeking answers for years to come. Elias had sought out the books of the Bible that referenced angels to try to understand what these ancient theologians-philosophers were interpreting in their older works. And he wanted to see how they all tied in with theories about aliens visiting earth. No matter what the Roman Catholic Church taught, Elias believed and questioned it at the same time. Angels and aliens were no exceptions.

He found numerous references to angels in the Old Testament. Among them were two in Genesis, where angels were the rescuers of Lot and his daughters, and of Hagar and Ishmael. And in Judges, an angel announced the conception of Samson. An angel again announced the conceptions of John the Baptist and of Jesus in Luke in the New Testament. They warned, ministered, rescued, and guided. In Matthew, one rolled back the stone from the tomb of Jesus and announced his resurrection.

Elias had also read a variety of other writings – the extra-biblical or pseudepigraphal works – that were not considered to be "inspired scripture," as the books of the Bible were. But, those writings had influenced Christian thinking, and so he read the primary writings on angels by the early 6th century Pseudo-Dionysius the Areopagite, and by the medieval 13th century Italian priest, Thomas Aquinas. He had also read many other works, in whole or in part, that fell under the category of 'false writings' that dated from around 200 BC to 300 AD. While they added greatly to his body of angel knowledge and other religious lore, he recognized that he needed to treat them with a very healthy dose of skepticism. So far he had explored the *Book of Enoch*, the *Book of Noah*, the *Psalter of Solomon*, the *Testament of Abraham*, the *Apocalypse of Ezra*, *Zechariah*, the *Acts of Paul*, the *Gospel of Thomas*, and the *History of James*. He had also read the *Book of Tobit* in the Roman Catholic *Apocrypha*. And there were so many others whose covers he had not yet cracked.

I need more time ...

Through all of his readings, he had been able to determine that the word 'angel' was derived from very ancient words in Mycenaean and Persian that eventually made their way into ancient Greek as 'aggalos' and then morphed into Latin forms such as 'angelos' and 'angelus.' Later, the Old English word 'engel' – pronounced with a hard g sound – and the Old French 'angele' appeared. Eventually, the word 'angel' became the accepted modern English pronunciation.

The word 'angel' basically referred to a supernatural being that was an agent of God. That agent could be a messenger, a rescuer, and even a warrior. And then there were the 'fallen angels,' the ones who rebelled against God and were expelled from Heaven – and not to be confused with demons which were disembodied spirits that walked the earth. Angels had celestial bodies, were immortal, and lived in the celestial realm.

Aquinas, relying heavily on Pseudo-Dionysius, had used Biblical passages to define a rather speculative hierarchy of angels, describing their various orders, also called choirs, a term which some angel experts purported was the meaning used in the line 'Sing choirs of angels,' from the song *O Come All Ye Faithful*. Elias didn't quite see it that way. It was a song after all, so he was confident that in that instance the meaning of choirs was choruses.

There were nine choirs of angels: seraphim, cherubim, thrones/ophanim, dominions/lordships, virtues, powers, principalities, archangels, and angels. The thrones were of particular interest to Elias. They were also known as 'ophanim,' a Hebrew term spelled variously as 'ophode' or 'ophde' (singular), and 'ofanim,' 'auphanim,' and 'owfanam.' They were also called 'erelim.' The word ophanim meant 'wheels' or 'revolving.' These were the elder angels described in Biblical translations of Paul of Tarsus in Colossians and of Ezekiel as 'wheels-within-wheels,' with rims covered with hundreds of eyes. Daniel 7:9-10 wrote: 'As I looked, thrones were set in place, and the Ancient of Days took his seat. ... His throne was flaming with fire, and its wheels were all ablaze.'

There were such images found in ancient and medieval art, and they formed a basis for the belief by some in earthly visitations by extraterrestrials. The ophanim existed. Of that, Elias was certain, because he believed what he saw with his own eyes when he viewed the images of these wheels-within-wheels in art from ancient cultures all over the world. What he didn't know, what he questioned, was what the wheels were by 21st century standards and knowledge. Angels? Aliens? Were they one in the same? Or could they have been early flying vehicles invented by and used by humans and then lost or forgotten over the millennia? Again, he believed, but he had some questions.

He had a lot of questions about demons. Even though he had studied them briefly when he was in school, he had only superficially delved into their existence and role in the spiritual realm. He was keenly aware that there was true evil in the world, of that he was positive. But was that evil the result of intervention by demons? What about the psychological impact of the parents on a future evil-doer's behavior? Surely the nature-nurture aspects of a person's life would have a direct influence on how they saw the world and interacted with it. Or could the parents be influenced by Satan or demons and then pass on that evil to their child?

He didn't know what to think about demons. They were something he greatly feared yet knew he needed to study to fully understand. He just kept procrastinating in that study because he was so afraid that he might accidentally unleash an evil demon on himself, or on the world.

Someday. No rush. No hurry.

CHAPTER 3

"I'm off to Venice Beach to check in on ... Johnson, Wynans, and Pruitt-Woods. I'm going straight home afterwards. See you in the morning." Donna Rodriguez slipped her purse over her shoulder, snapped her briefcase closed, picked up her jacket and car keys, waved to Gina the receptionist, and headed for the parking lot. It was only her first week working the West L.A. area after leaving the Long Beach office to take over the cases of the recently retired social worker, Linda Cicero.

Office visits with clients were acceptable in some cases, but home visits were a big part of the average case worker's job. And it could be frightening at times, especially for those who were new to this type of work. You didn't know who or what you might encounter when you knocked at the front door, let alone what you might run up against in the neighborhood. But seeing a client in their home was a necessity, especially if children were involved or the client was ill. And in Donna's case, all of her clients were mentally ill. That was her specialty area, and one for which she had extensive training far beyond her college education.

A home visit allowed a case worker to observe and keep tabs on the client's living conditions for safety and well-being, and to hopefully nip a problem in the bud before it had the chance to get out of control. Donna always tried to maintain a steady balance between authority and congeniality with her clients when making home visits. She wanted them to know she was in charge and that she was going to carefully look around their house to see if they had food, if the place was sufficiently clean, if everything appeared to be in good repair, and so forth. But she didn't want them to feel that she was their enemy, and so she also tried her best to be kind and helpful. It was not an easy game to play, and she had failed at it miserably in her early days.

First visits were always that hardest. Donna had been assigned 153 clients, and she had spent two days trying to decide which ones should be her top priorities. That narrowed it down to 39. She plotted their locations on a photocopy of a map and determined that if she could see a minimum of three per day, she should be able to get a handle on those 39 within a couple of weeks. Then she could start delving into the remaining clients who also needed her attention.

She was glad to be back on her home turf and finally relieved of the daily Harbor Freeway commute to Long Beach. She drove west in the heavy traffic that plagued Pico Boulevard. As she approached Venice Beach, she hung a left onto the even busier Neilson Way which eventually became Pacific Avenue. Once she got to Rose Avenue she turned left, and then right onto 7th Avenue where she tried to find a parking spot, finally settling on one that was three blocks from her first stop, the Johnsons. The area was much improved but still littered and dirty in parts, with weeds growing through the cracks in the sidewalk.

The Johnsons lived in a rundown, dull-green duplex wedged between two attractive cottages. Lingering at the front gate were three boys who looked to be fresh out of their teens. One wore a hairnet, the other a knit cap, and the other sported a shaved head. They barely moved enough to let her squeeze her round body through the cyclone fence gate, and one leaned towards her and whispered, "What's up, girl?" as she walked past him.

Janique Johnson answered the door. She was a grossly overweight, pimple-faced African-American teenager of 16.

She suffered from bipolar disorder and was under the care of a physician. Janique was also the mother of an adorable toddler, Micah. A child with a child, she lived with her diabetic mother in the two-bedroom unit. Janique was quiet and somewhat sullen, but she listened politely and answered questions, she showed Donna around the reasonably clean and spartanly-furnished space. Micah appeared to be clean and healthy. Donna considered this first visit to be uneventful but successful. One down, two to go.

She left the Johnson house and continued to walk south on 7th until she came to a small white house on a corner lot. Eugene Wynans was an angry, chain-smoking, 60-year-old hoarder who refused to let Donna into his house, and for that Donna was truly grateful. They instead stood in his private junk yard. It was an eyesore to be sure. She could see why the neighbors had complained and why the city ordered the cleanup. It was littered from fence to fence with everything from toys to appliances to auto parts to furniture. Nothing looked salvageable to Donna's eyes. She attempted to calm him down, but Wynans refused to listen to anything she tried to say. She would open her mouth to speak and he would promptly interrupt her with a tirade of angry words about not wanting the city to clean up his property inside and out. He waved a wrinkled court order in the air as he ranted about the government interfering in the private lives of its citizens. As she walked away, he left her with a few choice four-letter words and then stormed back into his hell-hole habitation, slamming the door behind him.

Donna felt a momentary rise in her blood pressure and took a few deep breaths before she made the walk back to her car. Someone should have been helping Wynans before things escalated to this point. She understood his psychological problem of hoarding. What she didn't understand anymore was 'the system,' even after working in it for going on twenty years. She felt a deep spiritual obligation to help others. That was why she chose social services for her career. But the longer she worked in the system, the more doubts and questions she had about its efficacy. It seemed to her that it failed more often than not, especially when it came to helping people who had psychological problems. Or, perhaps that was just her own particular bias.

A lot of the people in the system were mentally disturbed, suffering from any number of serious diseases and disorders, some simultaneously, and those were the very people Donna most wanted to help. Yet every day left her feeling more helpless, inadequate, and drained of every ounce of strength that was left in her 47-year-old, 50-pounds-overweight body. Her husband, George, kept telling her she should quit, sometimes even begged her to quit.

"Donna, my sweet girl, why don't you stop this?" pleaded George, his arms around her, trying desperately to comfort her once again. It had been another particularly difficult day for her and she had come home in tears, and not for the first time. "There are so many other jobs out there. And you are smart, you have a good education, you can help people some other way. Please, we – you and me – we have to come first some time, don't we?"

He was right. Donna knew it. But she was torn, just not quite enough to do something as dramatic as changing careers. And her inability to change careers had put a stranglehold on their marriage that grew tighter and more uncomfortable as her own frustrations grew. But a force inside of her drove her to stick to her original career choice. She felt there had to be a grander purpose behind it all, that God had chosen her to work such a thankless career because it was the right thing to do. And Donna always tried to do the right thing, even though the right thing was so often the hardest thing to do, the hardest way to live.

Her father had never understood what it meant to do the right thing, to live a life based on ethical principles. Alfredo Vargas – Fredo to those who knew him – had never done the right thing in his life. When he wasn't stealing cars and running a 'chop shop' in Inglewood, he was dealing drugs and running errands for low-life mobster-types like the Estrada brothers, Julio and Juan. As a parent, Fredo was a dismal failure. Her mother Esther, or 'Essie' as she was called, endured his daily onslaught of verbal abuse and his monthly spates of drunken beatings. When she died in an automobile accident, she left Donna and her brother Steven to live out their young lives as Fredo's little punching bags.

Fredo also began to put his violent tendencies to work for local mob kingpin Emmanuel 'Manny the Hat' Eszterházy. It was hard to say for sure exactly how many deaths were a direct result of Fredo's skills with his fists, a knife, and a variety of handguns. He was a prolific liar and managed to shift the blame for everything he did onto other equally likely suspects. Failing that, he always seemed to have an airtight alibi. He was rarely in jail longer than overnight. But when Donna was 12 years old, Fredo's luck finally ran out and his unsavory career came to an abrupt end. As he was walking to his car from a restaurant in San Pedro, he was shot and killed by the late Julio Estrada's son, Javier. The police believed it was revenge for the death of Julio, and Donna didn't doubt for even a second that Fredo had, in fact, killed Julio, probably with his bare hands.

With no living relatives except an elderly and infirmed great-aunt in Fresno, Donna and Steven were thrown into different foster care homes. Steven was only 9, and he bounced around from one home to another, rarely staying in one place longer than six months. When he finally aged out of the foster system, it was clear that he was destined to continue that erratic pattern in the prison system. And he did. Steven took after his father as far as a life of crime was concerned. But unlike his father, Steven spent most of his life in and out of jail, most recently for armed robbery. He was currently serving the last two years of a nine-year sentence at the California State Prison in Lancaster. There was little hope that Steven would ever be paroled. He showed no remorse for what he had done, and showed no evidence of trying to rehabilitate himself.

The Lord helps those who help themselves.

When Donna saw him three years earlier, all he could talk about was getting out so that he could accept a job from yet another local criminal. She gave up trying to talk sense into the rock-hard skull of her hot-headed brother, and she eventually stopped visiting altogether. As far as she could tell, Steven was destined to be a career criminal, and she would pray daily for his soul throughout the rest of her life.

Unlike her wayward brother, Donna's life in foster care was a tremendous success story. Her first and only home was with a devout Catholic family, Simon and Grace Arco, their two teenagers, Rowan and Maya, and a host of other relatives who almost instantly embraced Donna as one of their own. On her 15th birthday, Simon and Grace officially adopted her, and she loved them as passionately as any child could love its biological parents. Her relationships with all the Arco family members were strong, and she saw them all regularly, including most holidays, which she alternated each year in order to also spend time with her husband's family.

With the love and support of all the Arcos, Donna finished high school and enrolled at California State University at Northridge. She obtained her bachelor's degree in Social Science and then went on to complete a master's degree in Social Work. It was during her first year in college, before she had even an inkling of what she wanted to study, that she began volunteering in the beachfront communities of West Los Angeles.

It started with the homeless at the St. Joseph Center in Venice. She had been volunteering there for only three weeks when she began to see her future quite clearly. She was raised by the Arcos to do the right thing in life. Everyone in the family lived by that precept. It was in keeping with their spiritual beliefs, the ones originally installed in Donna by her mother and then nurtured in her over the years by the Arco family. And for Donna, those beliefs meant helping those who couldn't help themselves. The way the Arcos had helped her.

Now, all these years later, Donna was older and wiser, and with the exception of a few months in her early teens when she wanted to be a nun, she had never once doubted for a split-second her career choice in social services. But, just because she chose that career field didn't mean she wasn't frequently frustrated or angry with the work situations in which her hands were so firmly tied, often leaving her feeling completely helpless and ineffective as she desperately fought to make a difference. If only she could successfully and simultaneously work the system *and* make the system work.

The problem – the gargantuan problem – was that there were so many different problems. If it was only a single problem, then it would not be a problem at all, because a single solution would fix the problem for everyone. But that was not the case. The problems were so varied and the causes so diverse. She learned a lot about problem-solving while volunteering with the homeless.

No two homeless people were alike. The causes of homelessness were legion. When most people thought about homeless people – if they thought about them at all – they pictured the mentally ill people who acted out on the streets. But, the truth was that far more people were homeless due to physical illness than any other reason, and sometimes those physical illnesses gave rise to the mental ones.

Homelessness was not limited to men either, although they were more visible on the streets. The numbers of homeless women and children were ever on the rise. And they were the ones Donna was most concerned about. She never ceased to marvel at the many questionable or downright dangerous situations in which women of all ages so often found themselves and were unable to escape or too afraid to seek help. She had only to think of her late mother and the brutality she endured at the hands of her husband Fredo. But nowadays Donna routinely met teenage mothers, battered wives, runaway teen prostitutes, and mothers of molested children who still lived with the molester-husband while their children were in foster care. She even had some experience with a handful of homeless women in Beverly Hills.

But the people that Donna was working with now were not living in Beverly Hills. They were not even homeless. They were mentally ill people who were supported by the system while living in the West Los Angeles and beach communities. After reviewing most of the case files she inherited from Linda Cicero, Donna quickly saw that more than half of them were located in Venice Beach, and while real estate experts could attest to the fact that Venice was a neighborhood on the upswing, it was still one of the last remaining havens for the poor and disenfranchised of Los Angeles County. The boardwalk attracted millions of tourists who in turn attracted thousands of homeless panhandlers – and predators.

Venice was an interesting place all right. It had been founded as a resort city in 1905 by Abbot Kinney, who created several miles of canals reminiscent of the city in Italy after which the area was named. Most of those canals had been paved over after Venice became a part of the city of Los Angeles in the 1920s. But Venice didn't die. Instead, it went on to play a significant role in the development of art, literature, and music. The Beat Generation called it home in the 1950s; Jim Morrison and The Doors put it on the map in the 1960s; body-builders began to sing its praises in the 1970s; the 1980s rang in the era of art and street performers; the gangs called it home in the 1990s; and it had been a popular place to shoot a film since the era of silent movies.

Deemed the second largest tourist attraction in southern California after Disneyland, an estimated 17 million visitors flocked to the Venice beach and boardwalk every year. Venice had now been in transition for more than a decade, and an estimated 70% of all its residents were renters, while hundred-year-old fixer-uppers were selling for $1 million and up.

The Wynans house was definitely not a million dollar residence, and it would take a lot of fixing up to make it truly habitable. After leaving there, Donna drove around and around until she finally found a parking spot on 'Little Main,' a narrow street that ran parallel to Main Street. Little Main was only a few blocks long and was next to a parking lot and right across from the well-known 'Binocular Building' that now housed the Los Angeles offices of tech industry giant, Google. Little Main was the closest she could get to the Pruitt-Woods residence which was on a walk-street or sidewalk street that led to the boardwalk.

She remained in her car long enough to open the client file marked 'File 2 of 2.' It was painfully thin as case files go. She glanced at her predecessor's rambling notes about Amanda Woods and her mother, Rhoda Pruitt, who had a long history of drinking and health issues. There was no mention made of a husband or a father of Amanda. Amanda was a diagnosed paranoid schizophrenic, and Cicero had made a few inroads to Amanda through the woman's cousin, Kimberly Brady. But, it seemed that Kimberly could only do so much. Apparently Amanda had a mind of her own, such as it was.

Feeling like she had a good idea of what was ahead of her, Donna got out of the car and headed south to the Paloma Avenue walk-street and turned right. Then she dodged traffic on busy Pacific Avenue as she jaywalked to the other side. She continued down Paloma and was more than halfway down the block when she found that the house number she was seeking matched a once beautiful but now pitifully run-down, two-story Victorian with dull white flaking paint, equally flaking black trim, and ragged lacy curtains framing the wide front window. There was a rickety once-white picket fence and the gate stuck a little, but Donna managed to open it and close the latch behind her. She walked down the short path through the miniature front yard filled with overgrown shrubs and dense grass and weeds that grew higher than her knees.

She walked up the steps onto the sagging wood front porch that creaked as she approached the front door. She knocked on the wooden frame of the well-worn antique screen door. There was no answer, and she looked around for a doorbell and saw that it had been removed, its wires covered with black electrical tape that stuck out of the wall. She knocked again, this time harder. Still no answer. She walked over to a dilapidated set of faded wicker furniture that was in front of a large window and tried to look inside. All she could see was a sofa, a chair, and an old television set, but no sign of either woman.

It was summer and would remain light for a few more hours, but as workdays went, it was getting late and Pruitt-Woods was her last stop, so she walked to the east side of the house and down a narrow breezeway that was cold thanks to a stiff ocean breeze drafting through it. She came to a kitchen window and tried to look in, but couldn't see in at all because it was a little too high off the ground for her 5'4" frame to reach. But the door next to it was ajar, and she knocked and called out.

"Mrs. Pruitt! It's Donna Rodriguez from Social Services."

"Yeah, so what do you want?" came a snarling voice from behind her. "Where's the other one?"

Donna turned to see a thin woman of about 60, barefooted, and wearing long underwear under a faded denim skirt. Her graying hair was a haphazard array of uneven layers and her face was sallow and drawn, although it was clear that, like her house, she had probably once been very beautiful. She was walking towards Donna along the breezeway from the rear of the house.

"I'm your new case worker. Mrs. Cicero has retired."

"Well, I don't need a case worker, so you can go back where you came from."

"Mrs. Pruitt – "

"I'm Amanda Woods!" she said, raising her voice. "Rhoda Pruitt is my mother," she said in a softer but emphatic voice.

"I see," continued Donna. "I have been ordered by the court to help you in any way I can, to get you and your mother proper medical treatment, to make sure you have enough to eat – "

"I eat just fine. You can go now. I have company."

The door banged shut in Donna's face, missing her nose by no more than an inch. She stood silent for a moment, listening at the door, searching for some insight into what was going on. The woman said she had company, but Donna hadn't seen anyone when she looked in the front window, and Ms. Woods didn't appear to be dressed for company. Then again, this was Venice Beach, so maybe she *was* dressed for company. In this area it was often hard to tell. She decided to call it a day and return the following week to see if she could make a better impression.

CHAPTER 4

Amanda sat down in the overstuffed blue chair and put her feet up on the ottoman. She looked at the painting that hung above the sofa. It was a moody landscape with tall trees, a night sky, and a half-moon reflecting off a dark stream. She hid there once when the Benzos next door were having a battle for control of the universe. The female Benzo was standing at her window, and she opened her mouth wide, as if she were yelling, but no sound came out, only a stream of Benzo molecules that stuck to the side of the house and covered the window next to the TV. Amanda had escaped from it all into the beauty and tranquility of that miniature moonlit world. She stayed there for a long time. Days, in fact.

She wanted to go there now, to get away from this new Benzo woman and the pain in her brain. It felt like her head was going to explode. What had this Donna person done to that other Benzo nuisance, Lucy or Linda or whatever her name was. Mrs. Cicero. Right. That was her name. Linda Cicero. Why did she keep forgetting peoples' names?

It didn't matter what their names were. This Donna was merely another Linda. They were all Benzos. The world was overrun with them. These alien forces were infiltrating and spreading so fast. You couldn't tell one from the other if you tried. Always sticking their noses in other people's business, pretending to help when all they wanted to do was infect you. And she knew what they were thinking about her. She wondered why they wanted her at all. Deep down inside they were identical to all the other earth occupants, the ones who called her a lunatic or a schizoid.

But she remembered her past. Not all of it. And not all of it all of the time. But she did remember. The days before the Benzos. The days when she lived in San Francisco, when she had a life. Before she moved to Venice Beach to take care of her mother. That's when it all changed.

She'd been in Venice for too many years to count and had never managed to make any connection to it. It was extremely transient. People came and went with great regularity. You made a friend, the friend moved away. You made another friend and that friend moved away too. Or maybe they were there and she forgot about them. She forgot things all the time. But mostly people moved. It was always that way. The workplace was like that too. You got a great job, did great work, and then for no apparent reason you got fired and were replaced by the next new and better worker that came along. No loyalty to employees. She did great work out at Cal Poly, but they let her go. Said her absenteeism was a problem. She didn't remember being absent much. Maybe she was and forgot. Anyway, those problems were added to the high crime rate, smog, noise, traffic. Most of it was probably typical of life in any big city.

But San Francisco was a big city and it was nothing like Venice. Venice Beach could never feel like home to her the way The City did. She was sent to live in The City with her aunt and uncle, Margot and Ed Weston, and their daughters Kimberly and Annette. She was only what? Five? It was when Rhoda had launched into her drinking career. She remembered that she didn't want to move there, but she soon grew to love her new life, and by the time she was a young adult she knew her way around every part of The City. She made a point of going to exhibits at the DeYoung, eating piroshky at her favorite

Russian deli on Geary near the library, shopping for vintage clothing in the Haight, and browsing for something interesting to read at City Lights in North Beach or Green Apple in Chinatown. She loved to read. She would read almost anything. Poetry. Philosophy. History. Physics, of course, since she was a physicist. She still read a lot of physics books when she was not being tortured by Rhoda and the Benzos. She liked New Age topics too, and novels, especially science fiction.

When she was a student at UCSF, she lived with her aunt and uncle in the Inner Richmond district. She was hardly ever home in those days. Like most college students she was either in class or hanging out with her friends. It was in a bar called Henry Africa's at the corner of Polk and Broadway that she met her future first husband, Kevin ... what was his last name? After they married a year later, they moved a little south to the ever-foggy Sunset District where they rented a non-descript flat on 25th Avenue near Judah Street. She was working on her master's degree by that time.

His last name was Metz, that was it. She'd forgotten it for a minute. That marriage was not at all what she expected, and he was definitely not the man she expected. Kevin was controlling and oblivious to her needs. His influence over her was suffocating, whether or not he was in her immediate presence. And being in her presence was becoming exceedingly rare. Not only did he frequently fail to appear for dinner – or call to say he was going to be late – but he also made unilateral decisions that directly affected her. She felt as if she were entangled in a mass of vicious tendrils that pulled her in directions she didn't want to go, while holding her fast to a life she didn't want to live. She felt herself becoming increasingly depressed, and she spent every afternoon following her classes glued to the television and eating Häagen-Dazs vanilla and orange sorbet ice cream. She could never forget what that time was like. It was crystal clear, burned into the very fibers of her brain.

After fifteen added pounds and almost four years of married life, she had grown a new and stronger backbone and moved out with her two cats, Romeo and Juliet. She settled into a Victorian flat in the 1400 block of Waller Street in the Haight-Ashbury District, which was no longer the highly colorful neighborhood she imagined it must have been during the 1960s and 1970s, but it was still artsy and fun. She finished her master's and took a job at the university. Kevin had filed for divorce, just as she had expected he would, and she walked away from the marriage with nothing she didn't bring to it in the first place, except for the kitties. She loved cats. What happened to those cats? How could she forget anything about those precious little creatures?

The ink wasn't even dry on the final decree when she met Richard Woods. He managed a stereo store owned by his father. She met him when she went there to buy a new turntable. They began dating almost immediately and were married within six months. Hard to believe she was ever that spontaneous. Of course, she had changed so much since then.

She and Richard moved to a large apartment on Octavia and Sacramento streets in lower Pacific Heights. It was a gorgeous old building that overlooked Lafayette Park and it was a beautiful neighborhood, but it was a little too far from her work, and it was a little too conservative and traditional for her tastes – and now she was living in Venice Beach, about as untraditional as you could get, and she felt like a fish out of water.

She knew that everything was happening very fast with Richard, but he was everything that Kevin was not. Richard was attentive, he was always home right after work, and he never made unilateral decisions. In fact, Richard never made any decisions at all to speak of. He didn't like change, and not wanting any changes eliminated any chance of choices entering into your life. Ergo, limited decision-making. Friday nights, you ate fish. Sunday dinner was served at 4pm. Wednesday night was dinner with the family. Laundry was a Saturday morning activity, done the earlier the better. In Richard's mind, you stuck with what worked.

Or not. Amanda thought a routine would be do-able. She thought it would signify a normalcy in her daily existence, perhaps a sign that she was an adult. She wasn't crazy back then, but normal was still what she wanted. She had completed her doctorate and had moved on to a better job. That took structure and discipline to accomplish. But after four years of struggling inside of such a restrictive marriage, she said goodbye to Richard, filed for divorce, and moved herself and the kitties to a loft in North Beach. The only thing she kept from the marriage was Richard's last name, Woods, which she much preferred to her maiden name which was ... which was ... 'Crumskey.' Right. Crumskey. Awful name. Woods, now that was a nice name, and Richard wasn't a bad person, so she didn't mind keeping his name.

The North Beach loft was wonderful. She loved its old brick walls, tall windows, and rustic wood plank floors. Best of all, it had a great view. She was unbelievably happy there. She had lots of friends who lived nearby, including Georgina Castle, an artist and antique dealer who collected old mirrors.

She loved going antiquing with Georgi. She had started collecting antique blue willow dinnerware when she was married to Kevin, continued to collect while married to Richard and, after they parted company, she completed her collection of more than 100 pieces, all purchased one piece at a time from the many shops and estate sales that she and Georgi visited.

Whatever became of Georgi?

Amanda got a new job that was challenging and fulfilling, even exciting at times. She had completed her doctorate in theoretical physics at UCSF even though she knew it was unlikely she'd ever find a job in that particular field outside the halls of academia. Most of the available jobs in physics were for data analysts or data scientists. She was qualified for those positions courtesy of her masters in mathematical analysis, but she wasn't inspired to pursue them. And most jobs in theoretical physics were in the East Bay, and she wanted to work in The City.

Well, sometimes things didn't go as planned. She ended up taking a great job in Berkeley as a 'string theorist' at the Lawrence Berkeley National Laboratory. It meant she had to commute, and LBNL was not on the BART route, so she joined the thousands of people who made the daily drive across the Bay Bridge. It was a grind, but it was such a small price to pay for a job that challenged her. And, when she wasn't at work, living in The City presented her with plenty of things to do and great people to see. She had a real, honest-to-goodness life. A life she loved. For ten blissful years.

Then Rhoda Pruitt, the mother she knew by name only, got lung cancer.

She's your mother," said her Aunt Margot. "Someone needs to take care of her. I can't do it, and you don't have any brothers or sisters. It probably won't be for long. She's terminal, you know."

"I know, I know," she sighed, frustrated. "But she lives 400 miles away and what am I supposed to do about my job? I've worked hard to get where I am. I can't just throw it all away. Can't we hire someone to take care of her? I make good money and I can contribute to a caretaker."

"I don't think so, Amanda. Your mother is a very difficult woman. I doubt anyone is going to be able to handle her. It would cost a fortune, and you know I don't have much money, especially since your uncle passed away."

"What makes you think I can do it? I don't even know her. I haven't seen her for what – thirty-four years? Thirty-four years!"

"I understand – "

"No, I don't think you do. You're asking me to give up my life to take care of a perfect stranger."

"She's your mother, your own flesh and blood. Can't you get a leave of absence?"

"I don't want to get a leave of absence. I don't want to go to L.A."

"Please Amanda, it's for such a short period of time."

She remembered that conversation like it was yesterday. She knew she had eventually and reluctantly moved to Venice Beach. She couldn't remember if she took a leave of absence from work and they chose to fire her instead, or if she lost the job because she stayed in Venice longer than six months. But she went to Venice. She remembered that for sure. And then Rhoda defied all odds. She lingered. And then something happened to the cats. That's right, now she remembered. It was eighteen months after she moved to Venice. Romeo got sick and died. Juliet also was sick and she died six months later. Of course, now she knew that was the Benzos at work. Benzos made everyone sick. That was why she had to be so careful about eating right.

Month after month in Venice Beach turned into year after year. Now, here she was ... some years later ... she forgot how many, living in a dilapidated Victorian house with a woman she had once loved a very long time ago, then felt indifferent towards for most of her life, and then hated and loathed for who she was and the terrible things she had done. And all she ever did now was wonder why she came to Venice Beach at all. And why she stayed.

"Mandy!"

"Holy crap," she muttered as she gritted her teeth. "Go to hell, old woman!" she shouted, and her ears began to ring.

This isn't real.

"Mandy!" The voice rang out louder, so loud that it echoed throughout the entire house, bouncing off the tall ceilings in the living room and rattling the windows and the very foundations of the house. She could hear Rhoda banging her cane on the floor of her cluttered sanctuary as well.

This is all part of a delusion.

"Leave me alone!"

When will this ever end?

"I'm your mother! Come when I call you!"

"Fat chance," she muttered to herself. Then she leaned back in her chair as a wave of nausea swept over her while her head throbbed. She walked into the dark forest that was her refuge and stared blindly into the face of the half-moon. Like a lunatic.

CHAPTER 5

"If Linda Cicero isn't around to answer my questions about her old cases, where am I supposed to get the answers that aren't in her files?"

"Listen, Donna," began Gina. "I've been working here for almost ten years now, and everyone who takes over a case has to work with what they've got. Linda's in Mexico with her husband taking what is probably the only real vacation she's had in the twenty years before she retired. Until she comes back to the U.S., you're on your own."

Donna shook her head. "Thanks, Gina." She should have realized that being new on the job and taking over for someone else would mean a steep learning curve. She went back to her desk and again read through the files she had inherited from Cicero, this time more carefully.

Linda Cicero's notes were certainly thorough for the most part, sometimes overly so as the woman tended to ramble on a bit about things that didn't seem relevant. But her notes were also inconsistent in a few cases, and in four they were incomplete, or so it seemed. In particular, Donna felt like something was missing when it came to the Pruitt-Woods case. File 2 of 2 dated back to a case worker named Monica Baker. Baker made very few notes on the case, and her first and only action during her two-year stint was to order a psychiatric evaluation for Amanda Woods. The evaluation was performed by Dr. Karen Leeds.

Whatever led to the evaluation was not stated, and the evaluation itself was not in the file. All that was there was a brief letter from Dr. Leeds. It said that she had met with Amanda in the client's home and found her to be uncooperative, antagonistic, and delusional. Probable reasons were 'schizophrenia, schizoaffective disorder, or other psychotic disorder.' Leeds noted that Amanda adamantly refused a blood draw to rule out certain physical causes for her symptoms, but that aside from her 'outward hostility and delusional behavior' she appeared to be 'reasonably healthy.' There was nothing to indicate that Leeds had ever followed up with any recommendations for medication or therapy for Amanda, and neither, it seemed, had Monica Baker.

The next case worker was Carole Ruiz, and she rarely made a home visit, so there were almost no case notes at all. Donna counted five visits in two years. Ruiz stated that Amanda was hostile and that she regularly turned her away at the door on each of those few visits. Donna could certainly relate, but she suspected that Ruiz didn't put sufficient effort into learning how to communicate with people who were mentally disturbed. It was an art of sorts that took some time and patience to master, and the process had to be tailored to fit each client.

Then came Rufus Keaton. He worked the Pruitt-Woods case for almost five years before he was killed in an automobile accident. He visited monthly. His notes were not very detailed, and they were mostly about Amanda, with only an occasional sketchy and sometimes confusing mention of Rhoda. According to Keaton, Amanda was severely disturbed by her mother and the two had a long history of not getting along, and the relationship had deteriorated further after Rhoda was diagnosed with lung cancer and Amanda became her primary caretaker. While Keaton was on board, Amanda was arrested following a disturbance in which she struck a man in a small neighborhood market who was apparently harassing her and calling her names. Keaton took advantage of her brief incarceration to have her evaluated. The evaluation was performed under the auspices of Dr. Wyatt Kane, a well-known psychiatrist and currently an author of two books on mental illness, one of which addressed schizophrenia.

Kane's evaluation was nine pages long and included a somewhat limited medical history and a litany of blood tests that were all negative for any of the more common illnesses that could account for Amanda's symptoms. Kane noted her delusions and occasional memory lapses, her social withdrawal and hostile behavior towards others, and the self-neglect of her appearance, but also noted that her appetite was normal. His diagnosis was paranoid schizophrenia.

But Donna knew that it could be easy to misdiagnose a mental disorder like schizophrenia. Many symptoms of that disease could also be attributed to other diseases and disorders, including Asperger's syndrome, bipolar disorder, brain damage related to head injury, stroke, tumor, Lyme disease, and even the excessive use of street drugs. There wasn't a simple blood test that said 'Ah, yes, that's schizophrenia all right.' And that was truly a shame when you considered that it was estimated that there were 24 million Americans – 7 in every 1,000 – who suffered from the disease, and early diagnosis was key to helping them lead relatively normal lives.

For some people it was apparently too late. When Linda Cicero took over the Pruitt-Woods case three years ago, Amanda had been diagnosed with the disease eight years earlier. Of all her cases, Cicero seemed to take an uncommon interest in Amanda and her mother. She seldom visited Amanda, but when she did, she wrote long and detailed accounts of the antagonistic relationship between the two women, and of the arguments and battles initiated by Rhoda's rages at her daughter, and on more than one occasion at

Cicero. But still there was something missing. Something didn't make sense. Donna didn't know exactly what it was ... yet. But Cicero had managed to enter into the world of the mother and daughter duo, and Donna was going to do the same. She was going to make their lives better. She would succeed where all others had failed. She was going to be the one who finally made a difference once and for all. She would make the system work.

CHAPTER 6

Amanda woke up abruptly from her overlong nap and untangled herself from her afghan. She threw it over the back of the blue chair and made a beeline for the kitchen. She felt better after her dreamy respite in the moonlit forest, but now she was starving. Fortunately, the monthly check and food stamps provided her with a budget for many kinds of frozen meals, including pizzas and the little mini-tacos she loved so much. But she had to watch her figure. She didn't want to get fat like her mother did, even though she had become frighteningly emaciated after the cancer struck her down.

Amanda ate – that is, when she felt like eating – mostly frozen foods. Not only did they come in small portions, but the freezing process killed the Benzo molecules, the same ones that invaded her mother's body. Amanda didn't want them to get inside her too, so she kept the windows closed and tried to avoid being out in the world as much as possible. The Benzos were everywhere. They were always watching. They even came to her front door a few times, always offering to help her. They were next door too, and if she wasn't careful about staying away from the windows and keeping the blinds shut, they would spy on her, most likely to see whether or not she was on the way to becoming one of their many unwitting servants.

They already had her mother under their control, and they were anxious to make her one of their slaves too. But Amanda – when her head was mostly clear like she was pretty sure it was at this moment – was too smart for them. Unlike her mother who was utterly stupid and uneducated, Amanda was very well-educated and well-read. She had a doctorate in physics so, like most physicists, she was interested in everything, and she studied everything, often in depth. So she knew all about the Benzos. They squeezed in between the DNA molecules and turned humans into Benzo slaves. They got into her mother through her cigarettes, and probably from her coffee too. Rhoda smoked a lot and drank a ton of coffee. But Amanda didn't smoke or drink coffee. She didn't have to worry about those things. But there was still food, and hers was pre-cooked and then frozen, so all she did was thaw it out and eat it. It was much safer that way. Cooking released the Benzos into the air and right into the body.

Yesterday, at this same time, she had taken the beef stroganoff dinner out of the freezer and put it in the refrigerator section to thaw out. She now took another frozen dinner from the freezer and put it in the refrigerator to thaw in place of the one she was going to eat for lunch. She opened the bag and poured the contents into a bowl and placed it on the kitchen table.

"Mandy! What are you doing?"

Damn, damn, damn! Why wouldn't that woman go away?

It was pointless to try and eat. Rhoda would only continue to call her. She always wanted something.

Amanda stomped up the creaking stairs that led to the upstairs hall. Her mother's door was ajar and Amanda stood in the doorway of the cold room. She could hear the loud hum of the electric oxygen concentrator that was next to Rhoda's bed.

"What is it this time?"

I know you aren't real.

"They're inside you too, you know that don't you?" Her mother smirked, the cannula tubes running to her nostrils wiggling as she did.

"You called me up here to tell me that? Again? They are not inside me. Not now, not ever. Take a nap!" she snapped at the older woman, and felt her jaw clamp down on her teeth as she turned to leave.

"You're sick too, Mandy. The Benzos are already at work on you. You'll see."

Yeah, I'm sick all right. I'm a schizo.

Amanda glanced over her shoulder at the almost skeletal human body that the Benzos had commandeered. Rhoda's head was still almost devoid of hair, and only short gray patchy wisps were visible since her chemotherapy ended. Her cheeks were sunken and she sneered at her daughter, revealing her teeth, almost as yellow as mustard from years of smoking. She was missing a bicuspid on the upper left near the corner of her mouth and two lower teeth in front.

Amanda ignored her mother's cruel grimace. She knew the woman was lying, at least about the Benzos getting Amanda. Amanda was doing everything to prevent that from happening. But Rhoda was a highly skilled liar with years of practice in the mendacious arts. She lied like a rug long before the Benzos got inside of her. Lied about everything. Lied about everybody. She lied about her husbands, or was it just Amanda's father that she lied about? Or maybe they weren't lies. Maybe they were nothing but a bunch of crazy stories told by a crazy old woman. She couldn't remember Rhoda's stories very well at the moment. Everything seemed to run together and there were pieces missing. She'd find those pieces. They always came back to her.

She went downstairs to the kitchen and gulped down the cold beef stroganoff. As she sat at the kitchen table, she could see Klaws through the window. He was perched on the fence outside. She loved cats and wished he would live with her. He was a pathetic stray, but always so friendly. She wanted to bring him inside and clean him up, but Klaws was like all the other strays in the neighborhood. He refused to come inside. Soon, like all the other strays in the neighborhood, he would be dead.

She had read that most strays didn't live very long, and she'd seen Klaws on the street since his owner died ... six years ago?

Poor Klaws.

With that big lump on his neck he probably didn't have much time left. Benzos preyed heavily on the feline population in the neighborhood.

CHAPTER 7

After three years, Elias felt comfortable and secure at St. Lucius. He was always busy, but never too busy to neglect his academic interests in subjects that were peripheral to traditional church doctrine. They included, among many other things, angels, demons, and aliens.

But he was soon to meet, first-hand, a real evil at work in his own little part of the world. That evil came by way of parishioner Albert McKinney's wife of 32 years, Margaret-Marie.

"She's possessed by demons!" he swore, his eyes wide with fear. McKinney was a local farmer, a practical man who kept to himself, lived a simple life, and was not prone to drama or exaggeration.

Fathers Ignatius and Elias listened intently to McKinney. As the man spoke, Elias felt the hairs on his arms and neck standing to attention.

"She stopped going to church last year. Dropped out of the Altar Society. I didn't think a lot of it at the time. I don't mingle much, and I'm not much of a church-goer myself. But then a few weeks ago, she had this big ceremony in the back yard and she burned the old family Bible along with her old catechism books, some missals, and her favorite hymnal." He paused and drew a ragged breath before he resumed. "She even threw away her two rosaries – the one with white beads that her mother gave her on her first Holy Communion, and the antique one with pearly rose-colored beads that her grandmother gave her for her Confirmation a few weeks before she died. And they were real close. I pulled those beads out of the trash and stashed 'em in a drawer in my workshop. You know, in case she wants 'em back some day when she's better."

"You do know that some people can simply fall away from God," interjected Father Ignatius. "Maybe they're angry at God. It doesn't necessarily mean they're possessed."

"No, it's not just that. There's so much more. That was only the beginning of it. We had two antique crucifixes in the house. Margaret-Marie re-hung them, upside down. I put them right several times, but every time, I'd come back and find them upside down again."

"Did you discuss any of this with Margaret-Marie?" asked Father Ignatius.

"I tried. It's impossible to talk to her. When I brought up any of this she burst into fits of rage, throwing things, slamming doors. She even hit me a couple times. And her voice – it wasn't her. It was this deep, harsh voice. You know how sweet and soft her voice is, Father. And the words that came out of her mouth! I swear I never heard her use those kinds of words before. I was shocked."

Father Ignatius leaned back in his chair, his elbows on the armrests, his hands laced together forming a church and steeple. He had many times come up against people who had become opposed to God or the church, and their language was often heavily peppered with lethal doses of profanity and blasphemy directed primarily at the Son of God, the One they had previously considered to be their Lord and Savior.

"And then it got worse. Much worse," continued McKinney. "She started speaking some language. I don't know what it was, and Margaret-Marie didn't speak anything other than English except maybe a few Latin words like you used to hear at mass in the old days. But the other day, I started to panic. I just couldn't take this anymore. Father, my wife took a kitchen knife and she cut writing and symbols into the skin of her arms."

Albert began to cry, and Elias put his arm around the man to comfort him, hoping all the while that the troubled man was exaggerating a problem that was probably not at all related to demons or possession.

Not demons. Please don't let it be demons.

"I didn't know what to do. I thought she was a little crazy at first, but now ... now it's something else. I think she's possessed. I really do, and I need your help ... to exorcise the demon."

Father Ignatius leaned forward and placed his hands palms down on the desk top. The three men were silent for a moment.

"Before we can perform an exorcism, we have to determine whether there could be another explanation for her behavior," explained Father Ignatius. "We have to rule out any possible medical or mental conditions that could be the cause. If it's a brain tumor, for example, an exorcism is not going to help her. So you need to get her to a doctor."

Albert left that day, and promised to take Margaret-Marie to a doctor. Father Ignatius didn't go into all of what was necessary to obtain permission for an exorcism from the powers-that-be in the church hierarchy. He waited until McKinney brought him a letter from the doctor giving Margaret-Marie a clean bill of health – as far as her physical condition was concerned – based on a thorough medical evaluation complete with blood tests and an MRI.

Albert sat down with Father Ignatius and Elias, and Father Ignatius briefly explained the exorcism process.

"In an exorcism, an ordained priest asks in the name of Jesus Christ that a possessed person be protected from Satan and summoned back from and out of the evil one's dark influence."

"So it's one of the church sacraments?" asked McKinney.

"No, not quite. It's called a "sacramental," a sacrament-like ritual that's allowed by church canons, but only with special permission."

McKinney seemed to understand, but Father Ignatius knew that it was not as simple as he was making it sound to his parishioner. It was not anywhere even approaching a routine practice the way one would be led to believe from all the movies that featured them. It took Father Ignatius two weeks to navigate the church bureaucracy and receive authorization from the local bishop to perform an exorcism.

And then, he turned over the job to his devout but unwitting novice priestling, Father Elias.

"I have never done anything like this before," declared Elias, the tension causing his voice to rise an octave above normal.

"I will teach you the basic rituals of exorcism, and the rest is between you, God, Margaret-Marie, and the demon."

"Why can't you do it? I could assist you," fumbled Elias, desperate for an alternative to the inevitable, and plagued by visions from the old movie version of the book *The Exorcist*.

I'm only 33. I'm too young to die.

"An exorcism is for a single man of great faith, and that, my son, is you. I will be there, you will perform the rite."

"Surely your faith must be greater than mine, Father ..."

"Not as great as it once was, and not as great as it should be today," replied the older man. "But I was quite the priestly maverick in my day," he smiled, his eyes gazing out the rectory's office window into the array of oranges and golds under the bright blue sky that characterized a stereotypical East Coast autumn. "In those days, well, let's just say the church today would not have approved."

"But I'm not sure if I can ..."

"Of course you can. God never asks more of us than we can handle."

Elias was at once honored, humbled, and frightened. Over the days that followed, he met with Father Ignatius and did so much intense reading that his eyes burned from the strain. He studied the revised *Rite of Exorcism* as issued by the church three years earlier in 1999. It made the use of Latin optional, and he found it to be a more enlightened approach to the subject than he had expected. It assumed that the individual had retained at least some modicum of free will, and it provided a variety of blessings and prayers to use, in addition to a 90-page document titled *Of Exorcisms and Certain Supplications* and the section on conducting an exorcism in the *Rituale Romanum*. He hoped this new-found study would provide him with the tools he needed to free Margaret-Marie's soul from the grip of whatever demon had chosen to exert its influence on her.

But not once did he read anything that explained what a demon did or, more importantly, how to identify one when you see it.

CHAPTER 8

Donna Rodriguez felt the familiar sharp pangs shooting through her left knee. She had injured that knee several years earlier when she tripped and fell off a concrete step outside her back door. She did her best to ignore the pain. Most of the time the knee didn't bother her at all. But kneeling was one of those times when it did. And the longer she knelt, the worse it felt. But she believed one always prayed best when kneeling, and she had some serious praying to do. She was almost finished, so the pain in her knee would have to wait a minute or two for relief, which always came as soon as she took her weight off of it.

Oh Lord, please hear me. Please show me the best way to help all these people. Please let me be a conduit for all the good You do and all the miracles You work. Please, my dear God, please help me hold on to my faith in You and in myself to do the right thing, to make a difference in the lives of others.

A loud clunking sound broke the silence as someone entered the pew behind her and let the kneeler down. Like she ignored her knee pain, she also ignored this new distraction.

My God, my Savior, I know I am only a simple human being without the great powers You have. I ask only that I be a vessel for Your use. I welcome Your grace and Your love into my life that it may give me strength to do Your will. Amen.

She rose carefully, trying not to irritate her knee as she did so. She lifted the kneeler back in place. She stretched her leg and exited the pew, genuflecting only slightly and crossing herself before the altar as she left the church.

It was a hot Wednesday in August and the sun was ablaze at 1:30 p.m. Donna had spent the morning at the courthouse on behalf of one of her clients, a recovering substance abuser, and before her day was over, she had two home visits to make: Wynans and Pruitt-Woods. She had been working on a tactic that she hoped would get her into the Pruitt-Woods house. She had found a reference to it in Rufus Keaton's notes. After a few unsuccessful tries to gain entry, he had brought a fruit basket and flowers. Donna was going to do the same. She picked up fruit and flowers at the Farmer's Market in Santa Monica and headed for Venice Beach.

Her first stop was Wynans. Eugene Wynans was in deep trouble with the city. A crew of seven people was crouched down behind a 10-yard construction dumpster, waiting to clean out his yard. They were then scheduled to return again in thirty days to clean out the interior of his house. Wynans stood on his front porch, shotgun in hand, and the police had cleared the area of all but the helpless crew behind the dumpster. Donna pulled up behind a police car and identified herself as his case worker.

"He's been standing there for almost thirty minutes. We don't want to shoot him. We want to disarm him," said a young uniformed officer.

Another officer had a bullhorn and tried to convince Wynans that they had an order to remove him from the premises if he did not allow the crew to clean out the yard. Wynans stood firm, unspeaking.

"Do you want to try to talk to him?" asked the officer, handing Donna the bullhorn.

Donna didn't have enough of a relationship with Wynans to offer much hope, but she said she would try.

"Mr. Wynans, it's me, Donna Rodriguez, your new case worker." She was unaccustomed to speaking through a bullhorn. "If I approach could we speak privately?"

The old man lowered his weapon slightly and motioned her forward.

"I can't allow you to go there. We don't know what he's capable of doing," said the officer.

"I think I can calm him down. And I'm pretty sure he's mostly talk. It's his house. You have to understand how hard it is for a hoarder to see his stuff get taken from him. Please let me try."

The officer stood down and Donna held her hands in the air to show Wynans that she was unarmed, not that she thought he would expect her to be carrying a weapon. She prayed under her breath.

Dear God, please help me help this man.

Wynans backed into his front doorway as Donna approached. She walked into the yard and up the steps. He stood inside the darkness of his home.

"Come inside," he said.

Donna reluctantly walked inside and stood in the doorway where the police could see her.

"They're trying to take away my things," he said. And she saw that the angry man she had met only a week ago was now reduced to tears. "My things. My life is in these things."

"I know, Mr. Wynans. I really do understand. But there are laws in this city about having your things all over your front yard, and all your things filling up your house. It isn't safe for you and your neighbors don't like the way it looks. You enjoy your things, but they don't. In a neighborhood, you have to get along with all your neighbors, and that means keeping your yard clean. Do you understand?"

Wynans was crying in gasping sobs, and Donna truly felt his sadness. He handed the shotgun over to Donna and she took it from him, surprised at its weight since she had never handled a gun of any kind in her life.

"Can I keep some things?" he asked, wiping the tears from his eyes with a dirty shirt sleeve.

"Of course. There are people here who will help you sort through everything. But right now we have to deal with you and this gun. Do you have other guns in the house?"

"No, no other guns, and that one you got there, the firing pin's missing. Can't shoot anyone with it." He slumped down into a small chair in the narrow foyer and held his head in his hands. "When they clean the yard ... I want the sleds and the red wagons. They can take the rest." He was still sobbing slightly.

"Okay. I'm going outside and I'll tell them that, and then I'm coming back to talk to you. I'll probably be with one of the policemen when I return. Is that okay with you?"

The old man nodded, and Donna took the shotgun and walked it over to the waiting police. After much discussion, she and one of the officers returned to the house, calmed down the anguished Mr. Wynans, and waited for the Psychiatric Emergency Team to arrive to further attend to him. The clean-up crew was already filling the dumpster, and Donna instructed them to leave the three sleds and the six red wagons.

After the Psychiatric Emergency Team arrived she left for Pruitt-Woods. She held off on lecturing anyone about the lack of a support system for Mr. Wynans. Someone should have been counseling him prior to this extreme intervention. All her instructions had said for the previous week was that she was to mention that the place needed to be cleaned up. Someone had dropped the ball on this one. She was grateful that God had seen her through this poor man's crisis, and she hoped He would see her through her visit with Pruitt-Woods.

As she approached the Pruitt-Woods house, Donna saw children playing on the walk-street in front of it. When she went to the gate, one boy of about 10 years, walked towards her.

"You're goin' in there?" he asked, a look of astonishment on his face.

"Yes, I'm going to visit a friend," she responded as she put down the fruit basket and flowers and opened the gate. "Do you know her?"

"She's a witch!" he said and kicked a soccer ball towards his friends.

"Which one?"

"Which one what?"

"Which one is a witch?"

"Only one witch in that house," he replied and ran off to be with his soccer buddies.

Donna picked up the basket and the flowers and used her foot to close the gate behind her. She walked onto the front porch, hopeful that one of the women would come to the door when she knocked. But they didn't. She put her briefcase down on one of the front porch chairs and decided to go to the back of the house. That was where Ms. Woods had come from last week. It was unlikely that the house had a yard of any kind on the alley side, since few houses on the walk-streets even had enough room for a single parking space in back, much less anything resembling a garden.

She walked past the side door to the kitchen. It was closed, and she continued to the back. Another small gate was suffocated by mandevilla vines covered with vibrant cherry pink flowers. Donna fumbled around looking for a latch amid the heavy foliage and finally found it. As short as she was, she still had to duck to get past the natural arbor. On the other side of the gate was a pitifully short gravel driveway in which two vehicles were parked. One was a vintage dark green VW bug, and the other was a 1980s-style white Chevy Cavalier, its roof and hood covered with a fine layer of dust and sand, its front window reasonably clean. There was another porch and a door. On the porch was a washing machine and dryer, both harvest gold from the 1970s. The washer was churning, the dryer was turning. Donna knocked on the door and immediately heard footsteps pounding on the floor, growing louder as they approached the door.

"You again? What now?" It was Amanda Woods.

"I brought you this fruit basket and some flowers," said Donna, trying to appear very upbeat and cheerful.

Amanda looked at her and immediately reached out and gently touched one of the flowers in the casual bouquet composed of anemones, larkspur, asters, veronica, and some other flowers Donna couldn't identify. Between the purple and blue blossoms were shoots of sword ferns and English ivy. Amanda's eyes caught sight of the fruit basket and Donna could have sworn that the woman breathed a sigh.

"Come in," she invited offhandedly, not taking her eyes off the fruit.

Donna followed the barefooted Amanda into a room that was a cross between a wide hallway and a mudroom. Sweaters, jackets, coats, umbrellas, and hats hung from hooks near the door. Shoes, boots, flip-flops, and other footwear were neatly aligned on the floor along the hall walls. A box overflowing with empty grocery bags sat beside an old utility cart in a small windowed niche next to the door and overlooking the washer. There was a thick smell of bleach, ammonia, and other chemical odors in the air, but the house did not appear to be one where heavy-duty cleaning was ever a priority.

They ultimately arrived in a kitchen, one that was probably last remodeled in the 1930s. Had it not been so badly neglected, it could have been very quaint and charming. But the walls were an abstract mural of rusty water stains, chipped and peeling plaster and, on one wall, curling rose-and-windowpane wallpaper that was easily more than 80 years old. Donna immediately wondered about the potential for mold problems.

The floor was wide plank lumber – probably fir – but the cabinets and the walls were edged with the cracked remnants of old sage-green and black linoleum that had once covered the wood. Every inch of the tiled counters was littered with empty boxes of frozen food, and beautiful old blue willow dishes were piled in the deep sink and in a nearby drain rack. Neatly-folded newspapers were stacked in six piles, each at least six feet high, along one wall. The table was an old Formica and chrome model from the 1950s, and it was in excellent condition, clean, and remarkably clear except for a lone pair of salt and pepper shakers, again blue willow in design. Donna set the flowers and fruit basket on the table.

"How long have you lived here?" asked Donna, trying to show an interest in her client's home that might reveal some other relevant information in the process.

"Too long. Feels like always." Amanda didn't look at Donna as she began eagerly removing the pink cellophane from the fruit basket to pluck out an apricot. "Ooooh, I do love apricots," she said as she sank her teeth into one and the juice dribbled down her chin and onto her already filthy summer dress.

"Is that your cat?" asked Donna, eyeing a large brown tabby sitting on the fence outside the kitchen window.

"His name is Klaws. Not my cat. I feed him and other strays," she said in between noisily slurping up more fruit. "They won't come indoors. And they don't live very long. Always dying. Cancer, I think. Big growths. Mostly on their necks."

Donna didn't want to pursue that subject line further as she didn't want to upset her client – or herself – with talk of diseased felines. Instead, she shifted her glance to two library books on the counter and picked them up. One title was *Crossing Over: The Bridge Between Quantum Physics and the Paranormal* by David Atterbaum. The other was *Brane World Physics* by Cord Anthem and Michael Teeter. She glanced through each and realized they were far beyond her comprehension. She had barely passed introductory physics in college, and that was many years ago.

"Did you read these?" she asked.

"Yes," replied Amanda as she wiped away more fruit juice from her mouth and onto her dress. "I'm a physicist. Got my doctorate at UCSF."

Donna didn't know how to respond. Could this delusional woman really be a physicist?

"But you don't work in that field?" asked Donna, trying to lead her client into revealing more about herself.

Amanda started to laugh and spewed fruit onto herself and the table as she did. "Of course I don't work in that field. I don't work in any field at all. Haven't you heard? I'm a lunatic. A schizoid. A crazy. Pick your adjective. I've heard them all. I *am* them all."

"I'm sorry ..."

"Don't be sorry. It's all true." Her voice dropped off and she grabbed a dirty rag and wiped it across her mouth, then wiped her hands on it.

"I don't know you yet, so I don't know much about you."

"Not much to tell." Amanda paused and poked around further in the fruit basket. "I'm a schizophrenic, the paranoid type, the most common type, or so I've read. That means I'm delusional. I hear voices. I see things. And, the enemy of my enemy is ... just another enemy."

"Paranoid schizophrenia usually gets diagnosed later in life than other forms of schizophrenia. Is that the way it was for you?"

Amanda finished slurping on a plum, the juice dripping from her chin onto one of her dusty bare feet. "Yeah, I suppose."

"So you're capable of higher functioning than ..."

"Yeah, yeah. I've heard it all," she broke in, a little more than a hint of anger in her voice. "We're supposed to be able to live relatively normal lives. Hold down jobs. Have normal relationships. Blah, blah, blah! But I'm delusional most of the time, and meds don't work to control the delusions, the hallucinations."

The two women stood in silence and Donna again scanned the old-fashioned kitchen, looking for clues to Amanda's life, and Amanda continued to plunder the fruit, gorging herself as if she had not eaten in days.

Paranoid schizophrenics were not usually known for a willingness to discuss their illness, yet this woman did, albeit with some not-quite-so-latent hostility underlying her words. Donna wondered what behaviors Amanda might exhibit if her delusions or hallucinations were provoked in some way. She hoped the woman had not developed any violent tendencies that were not mentioned in the case notes. She wanted to continue the conversation, but the silence was suddenly broken when a voice called out from somewhere else in the house.

"Mandy! Mandy! Get in here this minute!"

"Who's that?" asked Donna.

"That's Rhoda. You have to go now. She won't want you here. Thank you for the fresh fruit. It's the only thing the Benzos can't infiltrate." She spoke rapidly as she gently pushed Donna in the direction of the back door, and the floors of the house began to rattle as if someone was banging on them with a very big stick or club.

The interview was over. Donna was on the back porch left with a myriad of unanswered questions. She stood and listened to the harsh female voice yelling and to the footfalls of her client, Amanda, running upstairs to attend to who? Her mother?

And what exactly was a Benzo?

CHAPTER 9

"Mandy! Now, damn it!"

"Stop that pounding!"

Amanda tore up the stairs. Her mother was sitting up in bed, her cane in her hand, pounding the floor. Amanda jerked the cane away from her, and threw it across the room.

"Mandy, Mandy, Mandy. You do have such a temper, don't you?"

"You should know, you old witch. That was the social services woman you drove away. She brought me fruit and flowers. You ruined it all."

Like you ruin everything.

The older woman adjusted her nasal cannulas. "She's a Benzo, Mandy. Can't you tell? No, of course you can't, can you? You're as sick as I am."

Amanda's mother was always sick and dying. She wished she would die right on the spot, this minute, and put an end to all the malingering. Or maybe, as she always suspected, Rhoda did die and this was a hallucination, a part of what she called her 'Rhoda-delusion.' Amanda wished she had the gumption to snap the old bird's scrawny neck and be done with it. But if Rhoda was alive, if she wasn't a hallucination, well, that would mean jail, and she didn't want to go to jail. The Benzos would get her for sure in there.

"I'm not sick. You're sick. Why are you still here?" asked Amanda.

Rhoda smirked as she raised the covers, pulled her legs up and under them, then propped herself up on an enormous stack of pillows.

"Well?" asked Amanda.

"I ... am ... your ... mother," said Rhoda emphatically. "You'd do well to show me a little more respect."

"Respect? You? I just want you to die once and for all and leave me the hell alone."

Rhoda snorted and adjusted the cannulas again. Amanda turned and slammed the door behind her.

"They're already in you, Mandy!" she shouted from behind the door. "The Benzos will kill you no matter what you do! They already killed your cat."

Go away, go away, GO AWAY!

Amanda clenched her jaw. It was so like Rhoda to bring up Poppy's passing, to make her feel worse about the loss of the little tabby she fed on the back porch for a year. Poppy was a pretty little girl with dark orange markings in a pattern like a watermelon rind. If the Benzos got her, it was because they gave her cancer. But she could have died from living on the street. It wasn't enough to feed a stray cat. You had to take it to the vet and get it vaccinated, and give it a warm bed to sleep on. But Poppy would only come to the porch and eat, and then she skedaddled away. As far as Amanda knew, the only thing the Benzos had to do with Poppy was letting her sleep under their house.

She wished she could go back in time to the old days. Most of the time she couldn't remember the old days all that well, but she knew they were a damn sight better than her world of today. She could recall different parts of her life before Rhoda, most of the time in considerable detail, but she couldn't remember things in order anymore, and she was pretty sure there were some rather serious gaps in her personal timeline. Gaps that changed from day to day. She remembered some of her old friends, ones she hadn't seen since she moved in with Rhoda back in ... back in ... she couldn't remember the year.

Whatever happened to her once best friend Georgi? Did Georgi move? Did they just fall out of touch? Maybe they had a fight? She couldn't remember when she last had contact with her. Then there were her two exes, Kevin and Richard. Yeah, that was them. Kevin ... something ... and Richard Woods. Of course, Woods was still her last name, so how could she forget that? She knew she hadn't kept up with them. Didn't much want to. She remembered her cats, Romeo and Juliet. She could never forget those two, not to mention any of the strays she fed.

Metz! That was Kevin's last name. Why couldn't she ever remember his name? She was apparently not having a very good day with her memories. Not that she often did. But today she was a lot slower and fuzzier. She knew everything was still there, stashed deep inside her cranium. She just couldn't seem to pull it out when she wanted to.

A sudden buzzing headache and a wave of nausea swept over her and she ran to the bathroom.

CHAPTER 10

The office wasn't open yet, but Donna used her key to come inside and start making notes on the Wynans and Pruitt-Woods files. She had a police report on Wynans and her own notes that confirmed it. She had also made a few brief notes on Pruitt-Woods before she left Venice Beach the day before. But Amanda had left her wondering. She needed to speak to an expert.

Gina arrived and the office was almost immediately open for business. Donna finished documenting her visit with Amanda Woods and then leafed through the file to find a number for the psychiatrist, Wyatt Kane, who had done Amanda's second evaluation. He was in Santa Monica on Wilshire Boulevard near Yale Street. She found his number and jotted it down as she looked at the clock to see that it was 9:45 a.m. Not too early, and after a short wait, he took her call.

"Yes, I do remember Amanda Woods. Interesting woman. Did you know she had a doctorate in physics? Diploma was on the living room wall when I visited. Paranoid schizophrenics are often quite intelligent."

"I saw her yesterday. She seemed normal in some ways, but she didn't seem delusional except for a reference she made to the fruit I brought her. She said it was the only thing that the 'Benzos' couldn't infiltrate. Do you happen to know what 'Benzos' are?"

"Hmm. I seem to remember her mentioning Benzos." Donna could hear him shuffling papers. "Ah yes, here it is. The

Benzos. They are supposedly aliens that invade the DNA of humans and enslave them with it. They already enslaved her mother, and they are also spying on her. She was very consistent in this delusion. She had some rather peculiar eating habits too, a means of preventing Benzo molecules from getting into her system."

"When did this start? Has she ever been on medication?"

"It apparently started when her mother became ill. Lung cancer. Amanda refused psychotherapy, and by the time she was referred to me for evaluation she was so paranoid that it was almost impossible to get a clear idea of what was going on with her."

"Did you meet the mother?"

"No, she was dead by then."

Donna was silent.

"Are you still there?" asked Kane.

"Yes ... I'm sorry, are you sure the mother was dead? I was there yesterday and she was hollering for Amanda from upstairs."

"Must be someone else. I'm pretty sure the woman died. But I don't have a copy of her death certificate, so I could be mistaken."

Donna thanked the doctor and ended the conversation. He said he had a few other notes on Amanda and he emailed them to Donna. The physics doctorate was confirmed. The mother's condition, not so much. And the Benzos? Well, that was obviously another story altogether. She went to the office library to try and find a book that covered schizophrenia. It wasn't as if she'd never dealt with the disease before, but she was now a little confused about the variations in paranoid schizophrenia.

She glanced through the pages of two books on the subject, and everything she read was what she already knew, that onset was usually in the late teens or early adulthood, but it could onset in middle age or later, and in some cases it could onset in adolescence but with slightly different symptoms. It was usually more severe in men than women. The actual causes were varied, and some pointed to stress during pregnancy or later, possibly with an increase of the cortisol hormone, also called the 'stress hormone.' The stresses mentioned included prenatal or infantile virus, low oxygen levels at birth, separation from a parent, and physical or sexual abuse. There was nothing in Kane's evaluation that mentioned any of these precursors to the disorder in Amanda Woods. Perhaps he had been unable to obtain that information from his not-so-cooperative patient. Or maybe the causes were different in late onset cases like Amanda's. But Donna didn't see any references to brain injury or anything that might have happened to Amanda when she was an adult.

But there was also no mention in Kane's notes on Amanda about some of the other more common symptoms of schizophrenia, such as the use of 'neologisms,' the invented words that schizophrenics were often fond of using. Maybe 'benzos' was one, but to Donna's ears it sounded more like a delusional belief. Yet in other ways, Amanda had appeared relatively clear in her thinking. Of course, paranoid schizophrenics were usually more clear-headed than other types of schizophrenics. And Amanda with her physics degree probably had a very high IQ, so she could have been even more high-functioning than your average run-of-the-mill paranoid schizophrenic. But she didn't have loose associations either, that rapid shifting from one topic or thought to the next, and she didn't repeat words over and over again.

She also didn't 'clang.' Clanging was a term that referred to a compulsive behavior that involved the use of rhyming or alliterative words that had no logical associations whatsoever except in the mind of the person saying them. It was found in a variety of psychotic disorders, but it was especially common to schizophrenics.

Maybe she happened to get Amanda at a time when she was not so stressed and was therefore capable of more coherent communication. Or maybe Amanda was on medication, although nothing in her file indicated she was, and Amanda had said "meds don't work." Next week would be another visit to Pruitt-Woods. She was going to make a difference. God was helping her and she would do it.

CHAPTER 11

The fruit was even riper and juicier than the day the social worker had brought it. Amanda stood leaning over the large kitchen sink as she squeezed the contents of a soft sweet plum into her mouth. She slowly swirled the delicious contents in her mouth and swallowed them. She looked out the window onto the bare fence of the neighboring house. Klaws was nowhere to be seen. Neither was the rest of the world, which was usually how she liked it. And today, all she could tell was that it was a very typical foggy summer afternoon at the beach.

If only it could be San Francisco fog.

There was a time when she used to go for long walks, even in the ocean mist. At first it was how she got away from Rhoda. Later it was how she left the Rhoda-delusion behind. It was during the first year that she started walking. She wanted to get away from all the demands: 'Bring me this, bring me that, do this, do that ... blah, blah, blah.' She hated waiting on Rhoda. She didn't love Rhoda, barely knew her, and hoped she would pass away quickly, as the doctors had said she would.

They promised!

To escape from her pitiful life as Rhoda's slave, she would head for the beach and walk in the waves, or walk down the boardwalk, all the way south to the Washington Street pier and back again. It was in those brief respites where she was alone with her thoughts that she began to notice that she was often forgetful and confused. Sometimes she walked along the remaining canals off of Washington Street, and on one occasion suddenly forgot where she was. Not only did she forget she was in Venice, she wasn't even sure who she was. But she attributed it to stress and continued her walks. In a matter of a few short weeks she had begun to recognize the homeless people – some by name – and all the various street entertainers – the fortune tellers, sword swallowers, and chainsaw jugglers. And the beefy and burly men working out in the area called 'muscle beach.' She went to locations where movies were being filmed and watched as they did one take after another of the same scene. She was glad she hadn't chosen acting for a career as it seemed terribly boring and repetitive.

But, no matter how far she walked or where she went during the day, she always had to return to the house to take care of Rhoda. The only thing that kept her going was knowing that it would all end soon. At least that's what she thought. But even after Rhoda died ...

She did die, didn't she?

She was never really dead, at least not to Amanda.

But she had a memory. It was a clear one now that she thought about it. It was early on a Friday morning. Rhoda had been sleeping a lot later than usual. Amanda left early and went for a long walk, stopping by the Post Office to buy stamps on the way home. When she got back to the house she found that Rhoda was not sleeping at all, but had passed away, probably during the night. She remembered feeling the cold, stiff body that was once her mother. From there on it was a blur. She didn't remember what happened next.

Who notified the authorities?

Was there an autopsy?

Who took care of the cremation?

The ashes were still in the house, weren't they?

She wasn't always sure about these things anymore. But she knew, or was at least pretty sure, that Rhoda was dead. She seemed to recall that her cousin Kim had confirmed that more than once. But Amanda couldn't always tell what was real. Maybe it was a delusion that Rhoda had died. Maybe it was a delusion that Kim said Rhoda died.

Amanda tried to remember when she first experienced the Rhoda-delusion. She thought it was the night following the memorial service. Her fuzzy memory and an oncoming headache were toiling together to block things of the past from her mind. Oh, right, now she remembered. It definitely was that night. Aunt Margot and Amanda's cousins, Kim and Annette and their respective spouses, had left earlier that afternoon. Amanda had gone to the grocery store, and when she came home she had a throbbing headache, was exhausted, and wanted to go to bed early. She was in the kitchen doing some last-minute washing up of a few dishes when she felt a small tremor in the house, probably one of those small earthquakes that were common to all Californians.

But what followed the tremor was a loud banging on the kitchen ceiling. It was Rhoda pounding her cane on the floor upstairs. No, not Rhoda. Couldn't be Rhoda. But it sounded so real. She decided it was probably the antique pipes, because sometimes they made a terrible pounding sound when the water was running. It couldn't be Rhoda. Rhoda was dead. Dead. Dead-as-a-doornail dead. But after Amanda turned off the water the pounding continued, followed by Rhoda's voice emanating throughout the house.

"Mandy! Get in here! Do you hear me?"

Amanda remembered that moment. Another memory, and a clear one, like it happened yesterday. Perhaps not the best analogy since she sometimes didn't even remember what day it was. But remember this she did. Rhoda, however mad she was, could never raise her voice quite that loudly because cancer had sapped her lung power. That was why she pounded the cane on the floor to get Amanda's attention. But at that moment so many years ago, she was yelling at the top of her lungs, and her voice seemed to be coming out of every board and nail in the structure of the house.

And so it had all begun that night. It was as if the old woman had given up the ghost, a ghost designed specifically for Amanda.

And a few selected others along the way.

She tried to put the Rhoda-delusion out of her mind, and she was sure it was a delusion from the minute she heard the woman's voice. Dead people don't talk to you unless you're crazy. Well now, that was a distinct possibility. She'd already had several lapses of memory over the previous year, and she thought she might be losing her mind or suffering from some form of early dementia. She was frequently confused, forgetful, dizzy ... She ignored the voice and the banging on the ceiling. They were nothing but a weird collection of sounds in her head.

They aren't real.

"Mandy!"

Not real.

Amanda broke from her reverie into the past, an apricot primed for her mouth held in mid-air. She took a deep breath and tried to ignore the call from above. The Rhoda-delusion was persistent and ignoring it didn't make it go away any more than did confronting it face to face, which she often did anyway, always knowing from experience that it would never end.

"Mandy! I know you can hear me. Don't you even try to ignore me!"

Oh, but I do try, and you have no idea how hard I try.

Amanda shoved the apricot into her mouth, sucked at the luscious fruit, and spit out the pit into her hand. It was almost time for *A Time For Love*, and she was not going to miss an episode because her Rhoda-delusion happened to call on her at such an inopportune moment.

The living room was littered with newspapers and Amanda picked them up and brought them to the kitchen where she put them on top of the lowest of six newspaper piles. She reached into the refrigerator and took out another beef stroganoff meal that had been thawing since the previous day. She put it on the table and took a spaghetti and meatball dinner from the freezer and put it in the refrigerator to thaw for tomorrow's lunch.

"They are watching you, Mandy!

She ignored the warning and headed back to the living room with her cold dish of beef stroganoff. She closed the blinds. Nosy Benzos. She knew they were there, Rhoda was right about that. Amanda sat down in her chair, put her feet up on the ottoman, and picked up the remote. At least that busy-body social worker Linda Cicero was out of the picture. She could have some peace without her telling her how to live. She could now watch *A Time For Love* and find out why Grace Peterson hadn't called her this morning. What was going on in Maple Valley? Was Grace still involved with Jack? Amanda felt an ocean of panic sweeping over her. She hoped her best friend had better sense than that.

"Mandy! Mandy! Damn it all, Mandy! Listen to me when I'm talking to you!"

Despite an encroaching headache, Amanda turned up the volume on the TV to drown out the volume of her mother's nagging voice. But Rhoda could out-yell the highest volume of any TV set. That was how hallucinations and delusions worked. They had no limitations. Nothing could stop them. Nothing.

CHAPTER 12

The date of the exorcism was at hand. It was a cool and rainy autumn morning, and Fathers Elias and Ignatius arrived at the 1788 three-story, cut-limestone house that sat in the center of a 36-acre farm. Albert McKinney greeted them at the front door.

"She's back here," he said, as he led the two men down a short hallway to an old-fashioned farm-style kitchen, complete with its original fireplace.

Margaret-Marie McKinney was sitting silent and still at the kitchen table and refused to leave the cramped room for a more comfortable area. It was clear to the eyes and nose that she had not bathed in recent memory. She was intently biting her fingernails and cuticles until they bled. Her forearms were marked with a disorganized mixture of pictographic scabs, her own hieroglyphic handiwork, etched into her skin.

"Margie, darlin', these men are here to help you," encouraged Albert McKinney. But when his wife's only response was a loud and prolonged hiss, he backed away, lowered his eyes, grabbed his hat off a hook, and reluctantly went out the back door, retreating to the peace and safety of his barn.

Father Ignatius pulled a chair from the table and sat down near the pantry door. Elias put on his short, white surplice and purple stole, and he performed the rite, adhering exactly to the words he had only recently learned, never paraphrasing a one for fear that doing so might cause the exorcism to fail.

He crossed himself and began, saying, "In the name of Jesus Christ, our God and our Lord, and made strong by the immaculate Virgin Mary, the archangel Michael, the apostles Peter and Paul, and all the blessed saints, and powerful in the holy authority of this ministry, we do undertake to repel the attacks and deceits of Satan and his demons."

Throughout the entire ritual of sprinkling holy water and laying his hands on her, and making the sign of the cross again and again, and throughout the endless prayers, appeals, and incantations, Margaret-Marie cursed him and cursed her God.

"Your god is a weak puppet," hissed Margaret-Marie. "And you are no match for the likes of me!" she growled.

"God, whose nature is ever merciful and forgiving, accept our prayer that this servant of Yours, bound by the fetters of sin, may be pardoned by Your loving kindness," he prayed.

The reek of death, decay, sulfur, and an oleo of harsh, unrecognizable chemicals burned in his nostrils, and he momentarily flashed on the old Biblical reference to fire and brimstone, the latter being an old word for sulfur. The room reeked of rotten eggs and became almost unbearably cold, then grew to an excruciating torrid heat that made him feel as if his entire body was engulfed in flames.

Margaret-Marie alternately laughed, snarled, and screeched, sometimes loud enough to burst an ear drum, or so it felt. She jumped onto the table top with the ease of a giant frog, where she remained crouched, defiantly waving her knife-engraved arms and occasionally lunging out towards him.

"Depart, then, impious one," he recited in a far louder and stronger voice that demonstrated not only his better recall of the incantations from so many repetitions of the verses, but also his increasing faith and conviction in the ritual itself.

Margaret-Marie only laughed in a low gurgling sound that erupted from her throat.

"Depart, accursed one, depart with all your deceits," he continued. "For God has willed that man should be His temple."

As he spoke, Elias drew closer to the crouching Margaret-Marie and looked her straight in her eyes. He saw that the whites were yellow. She opened her mouth as if to speak, then snapped it shut so hard that he could hear her teeth slamming together.

"I command you, unclean spirit, whoever you are, along with all your minions now attacking this servant of God, by the mysteries of the incarnation, passion, resurrection and ascension of our Lord Jesus Christ, by the descent of the Holy Spirit, by the coming of our Lord for judgment, that you tell me by some sign your name, and the day and hour of your departure. I command you, moreover, to obey me to the letter, I who am a minister of God despite my unworthiness; nor shall you be emboldened to harm in any way this creature of God, or the bystanders, or any of their possessions."

She moved her torso from side to side and contorted her body, bending her arms backwards behind her head and grabbing her own buttocks in the process. Elias wondered that her arms didn't become dislocated as her joints popped and cracked. She made a low growling sound and then spewed forth a flood of black ichor that landed on his face and collar, then let out a hideous cruel howl followed by a largely undecipherable spate of obscenities and profanity.

He was exhausted and felt he was failing at his task. But that wasn't at all unexpected. Father Ignatius had warned him that exorcisms could take days, even weeks. They had been 'at it' for a solid eighteen hours.

"Depart, then, transgressor!" he continued. "Depart, seducer, full of lies and cunning, foe of virtue, persecutor of the innocent. Give place, abominable creature, give way, you monster, give way to Christ, in Whom you have found none of your works. For He has already stripped you of your powers and laid waste your kingdom, bound you prisoner and plundered your weapons. He has cast you forth into the outer darkness, where everlasting ruin awaits you and your abettors."

Margaret-Marie stopped swaying and muttered more undecipherable gibberish followed by a wet hiss that was expelled from deep inside her. Slumping forward, she collapsed and hit her head on the edge of the Formica table top. Her eyes turned to glass, staring into nothingness, as a small trickle of blood escaped from her nose, and her lips moved as the evil entity that ruled her spoke.

"You cannot win this battle, Padre," it said in a deep, wet and gurgling groan.

"My Father fights this battle, and He will win," retorted Father Elias.

Margaret-Marie's voice suddenly burst forth.

"Father, help me!" she pleaded, as her body rose from the floor and into the air.

Elias tried to reach out to her, but as he did, and for a split second, the demon's face took the place of his devout parishioner, before it and its host burst into flames. He look for a bowl to fill with water or a towel to snuff out the flames, but there was no time. Margaret-Marie's body was immediately consumed by the fire and instantly turned into a pile of gritty, gray ash.

He remembered that moment as if it were yesterday. Two weeks later, he was on a plane bound for Los Angeles. That was twelve years ago.

CHAPTER 13

The late afternoon fog engulfed Donna, and she almost wished she'd worn a coat as she headed down the walk-street towards the Pruitt-Woods house. It had been a week since she last saw Amanda Woods. In her mind, she ran over the things she wanted to find out about Amanda and her mother, or maybe it was her aunt, or a boarder? She still wasn't sure who was living upstairs and she needed to find out. And she would find out. She was going to make a difference. She reminded herself all the time, again and again, that it was her mission in life to do the right thing and improve the lives of those who were suffering.

Oh my Lord, my sweet Savior, please watch over me and help me to find the answers that will help these two women.

"You're back," said Amanda when she answered the door. She was wearing an old-fashioned floral-patterned sundress that looked like it came from the 1930s or 1940s. It was faded and worn in places, and small brownish stains were nestled among the pastel pink and blue flowers. Over the sundress she wore a ragged, heavy-knit, pale pink sweater. Her feet were bare, and Donna could see that they were not just filthy. Amanda's toenails were an overly long combination of dirt, yellowish fungus, and ragged cuticles. Her feet were also dry and cracked at the heels, the way they were on so many homeless people Donna saw who were constantly barefoot. Donna tried not to think about how dirty the rest of the woman's body must be given the condition of her feet and the disgusting body odor that mingled with the chemical smells that permeated the house.

"Yes, I was hoping we might be able to chat for a few minutes. I brought you some more fruit." Donna made another offering, handing a small canvas tote bag full of apricots to Amanda. "I couldn't find any plums that were ripe," she said apologetically.

"Thank you ... I love apricots," said Amanda, eagerly eyeing the bag and taking it from Donna as she opened the door wider to let her inside.

The dominant house smell of the day was nail polish remover, and Donna immediately looked at Amanda's hands which, like her feet, had not seen a manicure in a good many years. The living room was small for such a large house, and it was dingy, dark, and a little messy. It was also in need of a good cleaning and a plaster-and-paint job. The faded, water-stained curtains on the front window were closed and a small circa-1920s chandelier was detached from the center of the ceiling and hung carelessly by its electrical wires. Donna made a mental note to contact an electrician.

Amanda led Donna to a group of two small raggedy sofas and a well-worn blue club chair with a matching but heavily-stained ottoman, the latter directly across from an old TV set in the corner under a window covered by dusty, twisted, metal mini-blinds. Amanda turned on a wobbly, vintage 1960s amber-colored glass lamp, sat down in the club chair, and started to eat an apricot. Donna took a seat on one of the distressed sofas and put her purse and briefcase down beside her since the coffee table was covered with old magazines and newspapers. She found herself facing a severely cracked wall on which a painting hung that depicted a forest and stream by moonlight.

"That's a beautiful painting," commented Donna, and she wasn't lying.

"Oh, yes, very beautiful. I live there sometimes," replied Amanda nonchalantly, her mouth bulging with fruit.

"You live ... ?"

"Mandy!" A harsh voice hollered from somewhere upstairs, accompanied by a loud pounding. It was the same voice Donna had heard the previous week. "Mandy!"

"Be very quiet and stay right there," whispered Amanda as she rose from her chair and went silently up a set of stairs. After a few short minutes, a door slammed, and Amanda returned to the living room and sat back down in her chair.

"Was that your mother?" asked Donna.

"Yes ... my mother." Amanda was eating another apricot as she simultaneously fiddled with her hair, twirling the greasy strands in her sticky fingers.

"Amanda, I have been reading your file, and I was hoping you could fill in a few things for me."

"You mean like a form, fill in things that are missing?"

"Yes."

"Okay, you ask me your questions."

"Mandy! What are you doing? Get in here this minute!" The pounding on the floor above was echoing throughout the house. Donna wondered what the woman could possibly be doing to make such a racket.

"Just ignore her," said Amanda calmly as she continued to twist her hair.

"It sounds like she's upset and needs something," said Donna.

"She doesn't need anything. She enjoys tormenting me. She'll stop eventually."

Donna was distressed over the loud disturbance. The pounding was unbelievably loud. In fact, it was almost impossibly loud. She'd heard construction work in downtown L.A. that easily produced an equal amount of noise. The entire house shook, and she wondered if it was structurally sound, if perhaps its decrepitude was causing the sound to be magnified. Or maybe the foundation had failed during the 1994 earthquake some twenty years ago.

Donna remembered that seismic event well. The quake had been centered in Reseda (even though it was called the Northridge quake), but it had reached well into other areas of the Los Angeles basin as well, and Venice Beach had received considerable damage, including cracking and toppling of many old chimneys. Perhaps the old Victorian had become unstable at that time.

"So, what are your questions?" continued Amanda.

Donna shuffled through the file, trying to ignore Rhoda Pruitt's calls.

"Mandy, Mandy, Mandy! You stupid child! She's a Benzo! A Benzo!" The rasping, throaty voice was angry and malicious. And Rhoda sounded demented, as demented as her daughter was believed to be.

"Go on, really, just ignore her. She'll stop."

Oh please stop, stop, STOP!

The pounding stopped suddenly, and was replaced by a low humming sound that seemed to be coming from within the walls.

"That's her oxygen concentrator," explained Amanda. "Please, go ahead and ask me your questions."

Donna was too concerned about Rhoda Pruitt to continue. She got up and headed for the stairs.

"You shouldn't go up there."

But Donna went up the stairs. The sound of the oxygen concentrator grew louder as she approached the door at the top of the stairs. She listened for a moment, then knocked lightly as she opened it. She was hit with a blast of cold air and the screaming of Rhoda Pruitt.

"Get out of my room! Get out of my house this minute!"

Donna entered anyway, fighting off a sudden and intense wave of nausea. She stepped over the end of a rolled up area rug. The room was frigid and the ceiling and walls were cracked and pealing. Two windows were badly broken and the glass was taped together. Spider webs criss-crossed the corners and shook as their inhabitants navigated them. There was a pervasive stench of something rotten combined with a strong chemical odor that filled the room and assailed her nostrils. It reminded Donna of a visit she had made to the city morgue to identify one of her clients years earlier. The smells in Rhoda's room were overwhelming and she almost turned to leave, but there, through the miasma of dirty clothes, towels, blankets, cardboard boxes, and a wide assortment of old and broken household items, was a rickety four-poster bed in which a small woman was propped up on pillows, oxygen cannulas running to her nose. Her face was severely wrinkled and her skin yellow. Her thick, dark steel-gray hair stuck out from her head like a crown of thorns. As she yelled at Donna, it was clear that she was missing some of her teeth.

"Hello, my name is ..."

"I know who you are. You're one of them. You're a Benzo. You got me and now you want Mandy," she yelled, wagging a bony and badly bent index finger at Donna. "I'm telling you for the last time, get out of my house!" The old woman reached for a cane that was lying beside her on the bed, and she began to bang it on the floor, making a deafening sound.

Donna backed away and again tripped over the area rug, almost falling over it. Behind her was Amanda.

"I told you not to come up here," she said, gently grabbing Donna's arm and drawing her out into the hallway. "Shut up! Leave us alone!" she yelled at the old woman, as she slammed the bedroom door.

"Amanda," admonished Donna. "Please, don't yell at her. She can't help it. She's suffering from dementia."

"She's not demented. I'm demented. Remember, I'm the schizoid. She's a figment of my imagination, a hallucination born of what is apparently my very favorite delusion."

"Amanda, she's not a delusion. I'm looking right at her."

"No, you're not. It's a 'folie à deux,' a shared delusion. She isn't real, and yet we both see her. Cicero and me, we were the same. We both saw her. She's annoying but she isn't real."

"She's real, Amanda." Donna opened the door and started to walk towards the bed, and the old woman pushed herself up into a higher sitting position. The house began to shake. An earthquake, just what they needed. Donna held on to one of the posts at the foot of the bed, and Amanda stood near the door teetering as the house shook.

"A folie à deux is not a shared *hallucination*. It's a shared *delusion*, a shared belief in something that isn't real. This woman is real," said Donna as the shaking eased.

"She is not real. Believe *that*," exclaimed Amanda.

Why doesn't anyone ever listen to me?

" Get out now!" screamed the insisting Rhoda Pruitt, with amazing strength for her visible condition.

"I'm here to help you," explained Donna. "I'm ..."

"You're a Benzo!" She shifted her gaze to her daughter. "See Mandy! It's like I told you! The world is full of them! They're waiting to take over your body!"

Amanda laughed loudly, a surprisingly shrill and hateful laugh. "You're not real! You go away! Go to hell where you belong!"

Donna was horrified at what she was seeing and hearing and could no longer respond. She needed to get someone more familiar with this type of behavior to help her. She was clearly out of her league. She turned around and left the room hurriedly, running down the stairs and to the living room. She picked up her belongings and ran out the front door. She didn't even try to close it behind her.

"Oh my dear Lord," she prayed aloud as she reached Pacific Street and looked for a break in traffic to cross. She was in over her head.

CHAPTER 14

Amanda stood in the doorway to Rhoda's bedroom. She reached in and picked up a small bowl that was sitting on the table next to the door. She hurled it at the delusion that was manifest in the form of a Rhoda Pruitt hallucination. She knew it was only the bowl that would be damaged – and it wasn't one of her Blue Willow bowls – but at least it was a quick and easy way for her to vent her anger at the cruel trick her mind was playing on her.

"You can't scare me away, Mandy!" yelled Rhoda.

"You can't stay here forever, you old witch. You've got to die for good!" She turned to leave the room as her mother's voice continued to torment her.

"They're already inside you, Mandy! You're sick too, and you know you are!"

"Words, words, words! Please stop talking to me!"

Amanda would ignore the words the way she usually tried to do. Although she could rarely drive the voice away, sometimes she felt compelled to fight back against what she knew was nothing more than a schizophrenic phenomenon. She'd had this confirmed by both Dr. Leeds and Dr. Kane, both experts in schizophrenia.

Dr. Leeds was the one who tried to put her on one neuroleptic medication after another. Thorazine, Haldol, Trilafon ... none of them worked to stop the Rhoda-delusion, and they left her feeling dull and apathetic. Then Leeds switched her to the newer atypical antipsychotics. Clozaril didn't do anything, and she was on it for several months, which made her worry all the time about the side effects it might be having on her white blood cell count. After that she tried Fanapt. Nothing. Nothing stopped Rhoda from invading her life. Each new drug she tried took weeks to take effect, and after long waits after that, Rhoda continued to taunt her and haunt her. Eventually, she stopped taking any medication at all.

From that point on, she began reading about different alternative treatments for schizophrenia. And there were a lot of them. Most sounded ridiculous to her, but most were also harmless, and so she tried them all. Antioxidants, vitamin E, Omega-3 fatty acids, niacin, a gluten-free diet, magnets, music therapy, art therapy, acupuncture, and Chinese herbs. There were other things too. Nothing worked, although some of them did seem to make her feel much healthier physically.

But there were still the Benzos to worry about. They weren't a delusion. Or at least she didn't think they were a delusion. She was pretty sure she had read about them in a book about cancer. Her mother talked non-stop about them. Or maybe she also read about them on the Internet. She was a physicist and physicists knew a little to a lot about everything in the world. And Amanda had an IQ of 178. She routinely read anything she could get her hands on. She had come across the Benzos somewhere. She was sure of it. She shuffled through papers on an old scratched-up credenza that had seen better days, and found her spiral-bound notebook.

Yes! She knew she had written it down. There was Benzo[a]pyrene and Benzo[b]fluoranthene. The Benzo[a] was a known carcinogen, and [b] was a probable carcinogen. They were found in cigarette smoke, charbroiled food, cooked meat products, car exhaust fumes, burning wood. The Benzo[a]pyrene in tobacco smoke caused genetic damage to the cells of the lungs – that explained Rhoda's cancer. The molecules intercalated in DNA and ultimately induced mutations. Then there were the benzodiazepines, the controlled drugs used to treat anxiety and sedate you when you were stressed out. Dr. Leeds had tried to put her on those drugs when Rhoda first began to torment her. Diazepam, or Valium as it was better known, knocked Amanda out completely. She had a good reason to fear the Benzos. And next door was where all the Benzos lived. A virtual hotbed of Benzos.

Amanda always knew when the Benzos were home. Their kitchen window looked in on her living room, right next to the TV. She could also smell it when they were home. And sometimes the smells lasted late into the night. The odors permeated the house during those times. She could smell sulfur, the stink of rotten eggs. Sometimes it was ammonia and bleach. Or rubbing alcohol. Sometimes acetone – nail polish remover. She had asked Mrs. Benzo what they were doing to cause the noxious odors, and she said that Mr. Benzo ran a small printing business from their home. Amanda did her best to keep the windows closed and sealed to keep the odors out. It was no wonder the cats wouldn't stay with her. They had such sensitive noses.

The house felt chillier than usual and Amanda felt sleepy, though only moderately nauseated. She saw that the front door was open and closed it. That silly woman, Donna, left it open on her way out. She was crazy too. Like Linda Cicero. Another crazy. They were schizoids too, exactly like her, and they were everywhere.

"Mandy!"

"Burn in hell!" she hollered in a sing-song voice as she settled down on the sofa and stared into the painting. A nice, quiet and calm walk through the moonlit forest was just what the doctor should have ordered.

CHAPTER 15

Donna didn't hear the alarm go off. She woke and saw that it was 8:30 a.m. She had slept for more than ten hours. Her husband George had already left for work without waking her up. She was glad she was married to a man who worked as a drug counselor. They kept similar hours, and he knew how stressful and fatiguing their work could be. That was probably why he so often suggested they both look for alternative careers, although hers was always the one that created the most chaos in their lives. He probably didn't have the heart to disturb her blissful slumber when he left that morning.

But now she was feeling anything but blissful. Her head ached from too much sleep, and she went into the bathroom to take some Tylenol. Then she went to the kitchen and started a fresh pot of coffee. She did her best to ignore the pain in her brain while she dressed. Before she left, she poured more coffee into her carafe and hopped into the car. It was 9:40 a.m. and she was late, late, late.

"What happened to you," asked Gina. "I tried to call and you didn't answer."

"I woke up with a headache and I guess I just didn't hear the phone. Sorry. That doesn't usually happen. I had an awfully disturbing day yesterday."

"Oh, well, I'm sorry to hear that. You had a delivery yesterday afternoon. I put it on your desk."

Donna went into her cubicle and wished she had a door to close off the noise from the ringing telephones and conversations going on all around her. On her desk was an envelope from Dr. Kane's office. She sat down and opened it. Instead of notes by Dr. Kane, she found notes from Dr. Leeds that had been sent to Dr. Kane at his request before he evaluated Amanda Woods. The notes were not particularly helpful, although they did mention that late onset schizophrenia after age 40 – and Amanda was in her early 40s when she was first diagnosed by Leeds – was more common in women and was more often of the paranoid variety. A long list of prescribed drugs and Amanda's lack of improvement taking them was also included.

At the moment, Donna was far less interested in Amanda's schizophrenia. She was more concerned about what she had witnessed the previous day between Amanda and her mother. Amanda had mentioned something about a folie à deux, a shared delusion, and Donna wanted to confirm what she already knew about that before she proceeded further in trying to help either woman. And she wanted to be sure she was not losing her own mind in the process.

She walked down the hall to the make-shift library and consulted a book on schizophrenia that she had referenced recently. It made no reference to shared delusions, which actually made sense to Donna. She instead looked around for books on psychotic disorders and finally found a reference to shared delusions in one of them. According to the definition and description in the book, and as she expected, this was not a shared delusion at all. It mentioned that to confirm a shared delusion, other psychotic disorders such as schizophrenia had to be ruled out. Since Amanda was a diagnosed schizophrenic, that ruled out shared delusions, although Donna was already positive that what she saw was no delusion, shared or otherwise.

It wasn't quite lunchtime yet, but Donna had skipped breakfast due to oversleeping and she was starting to feel hungry as well as agitated. She wished she had a pill she could take to calm her down. She was usually quite capable in the face of a crisis, as she had been during Wynans' confrontation with the police and the clean-up crew. She wished she could explain what it was she was feeling right now, this gripping pain in her stomach that was more than her appetite urging her to eat a snack. Something felt so terribly wrong in the Pruitt-Woods household, and it was wrong in a way that she couldn't define and she couldn't see a plausible solution for it as a result.

On her way back to her desk she stopped at reception.

"Is Mena available to see me?" Donna asked Gina. "I need to talk to her. It's kind of urgent."

"She's at the courthouse all morning, but she said she'd be back right after lunch. She has an appointment at 3:30 p.m., but the rest of her day seems clear. I'll leave her a note that you need to see her."

"Thanks, Gina." Donna hoped Mena, her supervisor Filomena Reyes, could give her some answers, some insight into the Pruitt-Woods case. Meanwhile, she was going to try to get more information on Rhoda Pruitt. This meant she needed to get into the archives and find File 1 of 2 for Pruitt-Woods. She needed to find out what the complete story was on Rhoda and what led to Amanda living there and becoming so ill.

The archives for case files older than ten years was located downstairs. The large storage room was lined with metal shelves and contained several aisles of shelving, all holding cardboard boxes filled with old files. She came to the P's and started looking in earnest for Pruitt-Woods. What she found was a file for Rhoda Pruitt, another 4-inch thick file, this one wedged between two much thinner files for Proctor and Pyle. She pried the fat file loose from its overstuffed box and hauled it back upstairs to her desk. She then went to the lunch room and got some cookies from the vending machine.

She returned to her desk, folded her hands, and closed her eyes.

Please dear Lord, help me to understand this problem I'm trying to solve for these two women. Please help me see the truth and the answer that will make their lives better.

She broke one of the cookies in half and popped it into her mouth as she opened her coffee carafe. She then began her examination of the original Pruitt file and was surprised to see that the case actually dated back some 24 years. The original case worker assigned to Rhoda Pruitt had been Lorraine Geiss, and she stayed on the job for eight years. Her original notes on Rhoda were lengthy and informative. They told a sad story, probably from the mouth of Rhoda herself, although there were several references to phone interviews with Rhoda's sister, Margot.

Rhoda Pruitt was born Rhoda Maxwell on November 26, 1937 in Oakland, California. Her father, Arthur, was a laborer who worked on building the Port of Oakland, and he died in 1974. Besides her younger sister Margot, Rhoda also had a younger brother who died in 1945 when he was a toddler. No cause of death for him was noted in the file. Rhoda's mother, Evelyn, was a housewife and part-time waitress who often left Margot and Rhoda with their grandmother while she worked. Rhoda quit school when she was 14 and took a job cleaning motel rooms. When she was only 16, she eloped with a former GI, Tony Ripetti. He was violent, abusive, drank heavily, and cheated on Rhoda. No further mention was made of Ripetti in Geiss' notes. The next thing noted was a marriage to Harry Crumskey. Rhoda was pregnant when they married and miscarried a few months later. Amanda was born three years after that.

When Amanda was 5, Crumskey was jailed, charges not stated in the file. At that time, Rhoda began drinking out of control. The authorities stepped in and Amanda was sent to live with Margot. No further mention was made of Amanda, but when Amanda would have been about 22, Rhoda somehow came to live in southern California where she married Ralph Pruitt, a car dealer, and moved to the old Victorian in Venice Beach. No mention of what happened to Crumskey. About three years later there was no mention of Ralph Pruitt either and Rhoda was working as a cleaning lady at a local elementary school. About 6 years later, she had a heart attack, along with other health issues, and went on disability. It was then that Geiss was assigned to Rhoda Pruitt and noted that Rhoda drank heavily, smoked heavily, and in general did not take care of herself. No mention was made of Amanda, who was apparently not living with her mother during the time that Geiss was Rhoda's case worker.

Maybe it was Donna's need to be thorough – she had been told on more than one occasion that she was overly attentive to meaningless details – but she wondered what happened to Rhoda's husbands. Surely they didn't all die, and there was nothing mentioned about divorces. She wasn't even sure whether or not there were any other children. Did Amanda have siblings?

After a few brief notes by the next case worker, Norma Gale, came a stack of medical records that started with a mention of lung cancer and ended with ... a death certificate! Rhoda Pruitt was dead, age 65 – although the woman Donna saw in the bedroom looked to be at least 80 years old. Cause of death was lung cancer primary and cirrhosis of the liver secondary. The informant was her daughter, Amanda Woods, and Rhoda's remains had been sent to a low-cost crematorium, the ashes to be delivered into the hands of the then-42-year-old Amanda.

CHAPTER 16

The telephone was ringing. Amanda could hear it all the way on the back porch where she was putting clothes in the dryer. It was probably Grace Peterson from Maple Valley calling to tell her what was happening in her life. Amanda was still concerned about Grace being involved with Jack and now with Josh Reynolds, possibly at the same time, although it seemed as if she had dumped Josh for Jack. Josh was obviously still interested in her, and they had history together. She wanted to know the real skinny straight from Grace herself.

Amanda ran into the house and down the back hallway just in time to pick up the receiver.

"Hi, Grace," she smiled, as she heard the familiar voice of her best friend.

"How are you doing today, Amanda," responded the voice of Grace Peterson.

"I'm doing some laundry, housework stuff, ya know. What's this about you and Jack? I thought you were in love with Josh."

"Oh, well, yeah. It's complicated. I still have feelings for Josh, of course, but I'm so attracted to Jack. I'm not sure where things are going with either of them."

"I understand. But I sure hope you can drum up the willpower to stay away from Jack. Really, Grace, he's big trouble. He's not what he appears to be."

"Thanks for the heads-up, Amanda. I've got to be going now. Glad to hear you're doing okay."

"Sure, thanks for keeping in touch, Grace."

Amanda hung up the phone and headed back to finish her laundry.

When she watched *A Time For Love* today, she would feel connected to Grace again after not hearing from her for more than a week. Of course, she didn't blame Grace for being out of touch. After all, she had two small children and a full-time job as a nurse at Valley Medical Center and she had to juggle all the problems of her relationships. Amanda could relate to Grace. She and Grace were both 35 years old. They even looked a little alike, with their long dark wavy hair and blue eyes. But Amanda conceded that Grace was the prettier. That was mainly because Grace had a much nicer nose than Amanda's, and ...

"Mandy!"

Here we go again ...

"Mandy! Get in here this minute!"

Amanda ignored the nagging voice as she removed the last of the laundry from the washer and put it in the dryer.

"Mandy! You can't ignore me!"

The pounding would start any minute. She knew it would. It always did. She disliked housework almost as much as she disliked Rhoda, but she picked up a broom and began to frantically sweep the kitchen floor in an effort to ignore the demanding voice that she could never seem to shut out completely.

"Mandy! MANDY!" The voice was louder, the pounding on the floor began, and the house shook as if an earthquake was rattling its foundation.

Amanda set the broom aside and walked slowly and deliberately down the hall, into the living room, and up the stairs.

"What do you want?" she asked the Rhoda-delusion from the doorway, knowing full well that she would not get anything new in the way of an answer. Just the usual Rhoda gibberish.

"What I always want, you stupid child. Look at yourself! You're sick! They've got you in their clutches!"

"Leave me alone! You ... are ... not .... real!" yelled Amanda, clenching her fists.

"Oh, I'm real all right, and so are they, the Benzos!"

Amanda tried not to react, but she desperately wanted the delusion to end. "You're an evil emanation from the hell of my mind," she said, shaking her fists. "And you're driving me crazy .. crazier. Go away! Go back to where you came from!"

Like that's going to help.

Hallucination, delusion or whatever she was, Rhoda Pruitt belonged in hell. She was many things in life, and among those things was a murderer. It wasn't Amanda's imagination. She remembered that conversation all too well. Or maybe she only *thought* she remembered it. Maybe it was another delusion too. No. No. She did remember it. Rhoda was alive back then, and Amanda had just arrived to take care of her.

Amanda had driven her 1999 Chevy Cavalier, fully packed with her cats, Romeo and Juliet, most of her clothing and other essentials, from San Francisco to Venice Beach. She parked in the back and had no more than set foot in the old Victorian when Rhoda told her to leave.

"I don't need anyone to take care of me," rasped Rhoda, sitting at the kitchen table, her oxygen tank in a cart next to her, the tubes dangling at her nose. "Go back to The City. You don't belong here."

The woman that was her mother did not look at all like Amanda had expected or like she remembered. Rhoda, who always seemed larger than life in Amanda's memories, was a petite woman who appeared to be no more than 5'1" tall. She was thin and frail, and had watery gray-blue eyes, a small, straight nose, and a well-shaped mouth. She resembled her sister Margot, but aside from her short stature, she was the very mirror of Amanda's face, just much older. Her head was covered by a bright, multi-colored purple scarf that was wrapped the way so many cancer patients did to simultaneously warm and conceal their hairless heads.

Amanda sat down at the kitchen table across from the stranger she hadn't seen for more than 30 years. She laid her purse on an empty chair and dropped a newspaper onto the table. Rhoda glanced over at the newspaper and didn't even look up to greet her daughter.

"We all agreed that someone should be with you during this time," explained Amanda.

"Well, I wasn't there when that decision was made, and I'm voting against it," she replied, still looking away, her gaze steadily fixed on the newspaper headline: 'Concorde Crashes.' She didn't appear to be reading it at all. She seemed transfixed on the news photo, and Amanda wondered absently if the woman could read.

Amanda had heard the news on the radio while driving to Venice Beach. Air France 4590 was en route from Charles de Gaulle Airport in Roissy north of Paris to JFK in New York City when it crashed into a hotel in Gonesse killing all the passengers, nine crew members, and four people on the ground. A front-page aerial photo of the crash was what now captured Rhoda's attention.

Reading about air tragedies was something Amanda didn't like to do. She didn't even want to hear about such things. They happened frequently enough that she knew the dangers and the risks of flying, and the Concorde crash was due to a fire in an engine on take-off. But she also knew that she had a greater risk of dying behind the wheel of her own car. She was lucky to have made it to Venice Beach unscathed given the traffic she had to navigate in order to leave the San Francisco Bay Area, and then the equally bad traffic on highways 5 and 405 entering into the greater Los Angeles area.

And now, after almost eight hours on the road, she was faced with a woman who didn't even want her to be there. She didn't know what to say to make Rhoda more welcoming. It was true they had no real relationship, and Amanda pretty much figured – although she never said it – that her Aunt Margot wanted her there mainly to see to it that they got to know each other better before Rhoda passed away. After all, once someone dies, all those unsaid things have to remain unsaid. It was at that moment that she decided to speak her piece, come what may. The worst case scenario was that she would very shortly be risking her life again driving back to San Francisco.

"Listen, *Mom*," began Amanda, sarcastically. "I don't know you, and I haven't seen or heard from you for eons. You abandoned me. My life as part of Aunt Margot's family wasn't a bad one in any way, but I should have had a mother, and you were never there. Never. Not once. And now, I'm trying to help you, even when you don't really deserve the time of day from me, and you turn me away ... again! You know, I tried to take a leave of absence from my job to come here to help you, and you know what? They fired me! So, are you really going to turn your back on me again? Do you care so little for me? Do you want to die alone?"

"You don't understand," said Rhoda.

"Then enlighten me," said Amanda, her body tensing and hot with suddenly feeling years of suppressed anger welling up inside of her, anger she never fully realized was there before.

"I don't *want* to die alone. I *deserve* to die alone," she responded, almost calmly. "You were lucky to have been raised by Margot. You would have been lucky to live anywhere other than with me. You're right. You don't know me or what I've been through in this life. I've done terrible things, and I warrant the death sentence that's been passed on me. Death is a fitting punishment for all I've done."

Rhoda stopped talking and Amanda furled her brow in curiosity, realizing there was an awful lot she didn't know about her mother's life.

"What exactly is it that you've done that justifies such a harsh penalty?" asked Amanda.

"I've killed. More than once," was the reply.

Amanda was shocked. Her mother was confessing to murder?

"It's true," continued Rhoda, looking into Amanda's astonished face for the first time since she arrived, and then again casting her eyes back to the front-page photo. "There's something terribly wrong with me, and it isn't the cancer, but I'm betting that the things I've done are what caused the cancer. You can't do evil and not expect evil to get you in the end."

"What are you talking about?" asked Amanda, her tone one of shear frustration as she leaned forward to be sure she heard every word correctly.

"It's why I didn't fight to keep you. I didn't want the evil in me to rub off on you."

"All right, I'll play along with this. Who'd you kill?" asked Amanda, resorting to sarcasm that sprang from her doubtfulness.

"It's a long story ..."

"Well, lucky you, I've got plenty of time."

Rhoda got up from her chair and went to the counter, pulling the oxygen tank behind her. She poured a cup of coffee for herself, not offering anything to Amanda, and then returned to the table.

"It started a very long time ago. I was only eight years old. It was not long before the end of World War II. My father, your grandfather Arthur, had enlisted in the Navy early on, and with three kids, he and Mom were kind of scraping by. It wasn't like it was during the Great Depression or anything. My parents talked about that all the time, so I'd heard how bad that was. Anyway, I wanted a doll, a Baby Beautiful doll. Our neighbor's daughter had one, and I had to have one too. I wanted that doll so bad. I don't remember exactly what she cost, but I think it was about $3, and that was an awful lot of money back in those days. And Billy, well, he was sick ..."

"Who's Billy?" interrupted Amanda at the mention of a name she didn't recognize.

"Billy. William Arthur Maxwell. My baby brother. He was three at the time. He was always sick, had asthma real bad. He had bad lungs, a heart problem of some kind, had pneumonia a couple of times. He was always needing a doctor. It meant we all had to do without even more when we didn't have much to begin with. He was the center of the world, my parents' world, that is. Mine, not so much. All I ever thought was, 'If he was gone, I could have that doll.'

"Then one night, he was coughing so bad. Woke me up. I went into his room, and I smothered him with a pillow. Just like that. I never stopped to think of the consequences. And there wasn't even a question about his death because the doctor figured it was his time, him always being so sick and all. But after all that, I still didn't get my Baby Beautiful doll. There were funeral expenses, and my parents had to borrow money from my Uncle Ed, and they were paying him back for years."

"You were a child," she said, shocked, yet trying to calmly provide an explanation and maybe even an excuse for the child murderer. "You didn't know any better."

"Yes, that's true. But it was only the first time. There was more," continued Rhoda. She waved the newspaper to the side and put her elbows on the table, holding the coffee mug in her hands. "Then there was Tony. Tony Ripetti. He was my first husband. I met him at a dance. I was only 16 years old, and he had just returned from the Korean War, honorably discharged. He was a lot older than me – 28 years old – and he was so handsome. Tall, dark, like a matinee idol. We ran off and got married after knowing each other for a week. But he turned out to be a womanizer, and he drank a lot, binges in bars. And when he drank, well, let's just say he got rough with me when he came home – if he came home. After a few months of it, I got an opportunity to do something about it. He came at me with his fists again, but I had his baseball bat. That was the end of Tony. I still have that bat, an old H&B – Hillerich & Bradsby – from the 1940s."

"How did you avoid being caught?" she asked, stunned once again. Rhoda was still technically a child when she killed Tony Ripetti, or at the least she was an emancipated teenager, if such a designation existed all those years ago.

"Timing is everything. I was prepared from the last time he went out drinking. We were living in a little apartment a few doors down from your Grandma and Grandpa Maxwell's house. They had a big yard and an old garage in the back that they never used. I'd gone over there several times, always when they weren't home – they used to go to a lot of church functions back then. One night, I dug me a real deep hole between the garage and the fence. No one could see it way back there. On the night I killed him, I got a wheelbarrow from that garage, brought it to the apartment, and late that night I rolled him up in an old navy blue rug, dragged him down the back stairs, put him in the wheelbarrow, and took him over to his grave."

Amanda thought about it and couldn't believe that this frail, bird-like woman could have done this without help.

"I don't believe you," she said. "You couldn't possibly have done that all by yourself."

"Oh, you don't know what I was like back then. I was very young, and I'd been cleaning motel rooms for two years, so I was very, very strong. Yes, he was a burden to move, that was for sure, but I also had adrenalin on my side."

"And no one ever found his body?"

"Not that I know of. And I removed all his clothing. Buried him buck-naked. He had an old 1948 green Dodge Coronet, and I drove it up Telegraph to a bar near the motel where I worked cleaning rooms. He used to go to that bar to drink and hang out with his army buddies. I parked his car about three doors down from the bar, left the keys under the seat like we used to do back in those days, and walked home. Waited a few days and then reported him missing. Nothing ever came of it."

"These murders ... they happened when you were still a child. You didn't know any better at the time," said Amanda, again trying to offer a reasonable excuse for such heinous crimes.

"But they are not the only murders. There is still one more and I was very much an adult when that happened."

Amanda's mind was whirling with all this information, and she was still not sure if any of it was true. It all seemed so incredibly unlikely. Her mother a murderer? She got up from the table, removed a mug from the drain rack, and helped herself to some coffee. She sat down and slouched back in her chair. "So tell me."

"I was so in love with your father. We were very happy together. After he died in prison, I started drinking, like a fish, as they say. And when you went to live with Margot, it was a blessing for you. Me, I went back to cleaning motel rooms. That's where I met Ralph Pruitt.

Ralph was a car dealer. He was going to some big car auction and he was staying at the motel. He was bragging on how he had this big house near the beach in southern California, how he was building his automobile empire by buying up antique cars and restoring them, then selling them to movie stars and other rich people, and even renting some of them to movie studios to use in the movies. I tell you, I was sure my ship had finally come in. We were attracted to each other, that's for sure. He went back to L.A. but came back a couple weeks later and we got married right then and there. Then we moved to Venice, to this house."

"So what went wrong?" asked Amanda.

"Men can be such liars. He told me he had money, that business was booming, and on and on. But this house was a wreck, even worse than it is right now. There was no mortgage on it and he had inherited it and its contents when his father died. We fought about money from Day One. I could barely afford to buy groceries most of the time. And he was always gone somewhere, hardly ever home. So much for my ship coming in. More like the sinking Titanic. Then one afternoon I was cleaning up in our bedroom and I found a locked metal box in the back of the closet. I pried that box open and there was more than $50,000 cash inside. I thought, I'm never gonna see this kind of money again in my life."

Amanda stretched but didn't say anything. Rhoda silently got up to refill her cup. When she sat back down at the table, she resumed her sordid tale.

"I knew exactly what I was doing. Premeditated all the way. It was wrong. I knew it was wrong, and I did it anyway. I deliberately broke one of the front porch steps. It was already very weak and creaky with a crack in it. I hired a man to fix it and replace the other two steps as well. After all the steps were removed and it was opened up to the ground, I told him I had to go out of town unexpectedly and that he could finish up when I got back. Ralph was in San Diego that day buying a car, and at night I dug a big old hole under the steps. When Ralph came home the next day I kept him away from the front of the house. It wasn't hard to do since he parked the car on the alley side and came and went from the back door.

"At night, after we'd been asleep for awhile, I woke him up – it was about 2:30 a.m. – and I said that I heard someone downstairs. He got up like a shot and headed for the stairs. I followed right behind him with the baseball bat. Tony Ripetti's old bat. Whacked him in the back of the head and sent him all the way to the bottom. From there, it was a short distance to the front door and the hole. I buried him that night and made it look like the ground was never disturbed.

In the early morning, I put on his coat and hat, and drove off in the car. I left it, along with his coat and hat and the car keys, at the airport in a parking garage. I caught a bus back to Venice. Like with Tony, I waited a few days and reported him missing. Apparently it didn't raise any red flags. The car was found at the airport a few weeks later, and the police assumed he'd skipped the country or something. That was the end of that. I didn't spend the money from the box at first. I didn't want to draw any attention to myself. Instead, I sold off some of Ralph's cars, and then I got a part-time job cleaning at Westminster Elementary. But I kept up what was left of his car business until his brother showed up and took it over a few years later. I was gonna fight him for it, but then all hell broke loose because I had a heart attack. All the money I had went into medical bills except for about $45,000 of the cash. I went on disability, and that's when social services got wind of me."

Amanda was at a loss for words. Her mother was a murderer and a thief. How did anyone respond to such knowledge about a parent?

"Mandy!"

She was ripped back into the present, and the Rhoda-delusion was plaguing her yet again.

"Please, please, PLEASE! Go away and leave me alone!"

I know you're not real!

"Oh, but I am, Mandy! I am very real!"

CHAPTER 17

"I hear you're having some problems with Amanda Woods," said Filomena Reyes as she motioned Donna to have a seat.

"Yes, Mena. I'm afraid I am in way over my head with her condition. And I'm afraid there may be something wrong with me or ... I just don't know what to think and what to do."

"Start from the beginning and tell me what's going on." Mena was short, dark, and impeccably dressed. She was known for being one sharp cookie, and she was always direct and to the point. Donna knew that her supervisor would expect no less from her. She gave Mena a full account of everything that had happened since she had taken over the Pruitt-Woods case. Mena listened attentively, never interrupting Donna, her brow furrowing from time to time as she tried to make heads or tails of what was going on at the Pruitt-Woods house.

"... and this morning I found Rhoda Pruitt's death certificate in the old file."

Mena nodded and swiveled in her chair. "There is probably a very rational explanation for this," she began. "The woman in the bedroom is not a delusion, shared or otherwise. She must be a relative or a tenant, and somehow Amanda's brain has twisted the identity of that woman into that of her deceased mother. If the older woman is sick, Amanda should not be treating her the way she does, and even if she is sick, she is creating a hostile environment for Amanda. We need to get help for both of these women, starting by getting the woman upstairs out of that house."

"Get her out how?"

"Evict her, find her a better living situation. I'll call the attorney, Marcia Silversteen, right now."

Donna returned to her desk and re-read File 2, looking at it through new eyes, trying to see if there were any useful details she might have missed when she first glanced at the file. She saw the initial report on Amanda Woods this time, dating from when she first entered the system. It was signed by Monica Baker shortly after Rhoda's death. It was a short history of Amanda. Born June 21, 1960. That made her 55 years old, although she looked at least 65, probably due to stress and her poor grooming habits. Her father was Harry Crumskey. Amanda graduated from high school with honors, graduated from UCSF with honors, had a masters and a doctorate, both from UCSF. Married twice, divorced twice. Single for a little over ten years at the time the report was written by Baker.

The person who had reported Amanda as needing assistance was her cousin, Kimberly Brady. The reason for assistance was that Amanda was behaving erratically and hearing voices. The next document in the file was the letter stating the results of Leeds' psych evaluation. Other than that, there were almost no other notes regarding visits or any other form of interaction with Amanda by Baker or by her successor, Carole Ruiz, who virtually ignored Amanda for almost two years, visiting her only four times. Even the next case worker, Rufus Keaton, had little to do with her aside from having her evaluated again, this time by Kane. When Keaton died in an automobile accident two years later, Linda Cicero was assigned to Amanda. It was from this point on that Donna realized that Linda Cicero was the only person who took a serious interest in Amanda, at least based on her copious notes about the mother and daughter and their combative relationship.

She had never read Cicero's notes entirely. She had started to read them, but they seemed like a lot of incoherent ramblings to her. She had read many a case worker's notes, and some were simply not as clear and concise as others. The first few lines were about a fight between Amanda and her mother. Now that Donna knew Rhoda Pruitt was dead, this didn't make sense. What was it that Amanda had said about being the same as Linda Cicero? The folie à deux, that was it. They both saw Rhoda Pruitt, or the woman who they both thought was Rhoda Pruitt. Apparently, Linda Cicero never bothered to read the first Pruitt file, or she would have known that Rhoda had been dead for ten long years before she took over the case. So who was the old woman in Rhoda's bedroom?

The phone rang as Donna closed the file. It was Mena.

"Marcia will meet us at the Pruitt-Woods house tomorrow morning, 10:30 a.m."

CHAPTER 18

The Benzos were at it again. First thing in the morning and the smell of ammonia had already wafted from their house into Amanda's. She hated that odor most of all. It reminded her of Silky, the cat that her Aunt Margot adored. When Silky was old, she took to peeing all over the house, including in Amanda's room. The ammonia smell of it was awful. She never liked Silky anyway, even though she was a cat person. She didn't much care for dogs. Her first husband, Kevin ... Metz, now he was a dog lover. He had a golden retriever named ... Max. The dog drove Amanda crazy until it died of old age a year into their marriage. Her second husband, Richard Woods, wasn't too keen on cats when they first met, but then he had no experience with them either. But he took to Romeo and Juliet right away and they seemed to like him well enough. She loved those precious little kitties, and she always kept their litter box pristine clean because she couldn't stand that ammonia smell.

Amanda went from room to room making sure the windows were closed, not that she opened them all that often, especially when it was so foggy and damp outside. And it was on days when there was no ocean breeze that the smells were the worst, the strongest and most potent. They hung in the air between the two buildings with nowhere else to go. It always made her feel sick at first, but she always got used to it as the day wore on.

"Mandy!"

Oh for criminy sake!

Amanda longed to have peace in her life. A few moments without noise, without voices, without strange odors, without ... without anything. She wanted to be able to think clearly again. Maybe it wasn't too late for her to get a job, if she could think straight. Drugs hadn't helped before. But that was a few years ago. Maybe there were new drugs now. Maybe she should go see a doctor. Maybe she should talk about it to the new woman, that new case worker ... Donna. She didn't trust her – she didn't trust anyone – but she was still the only game in town when it came to getting medical care for someone like Amanda who was on assistance.

"Mandy! Damn it, listen to me!"

She bolted up the stairs and burst through the doorway. "Leave me alone! Shut up and leave me alone! I'm so sick of you, so sick of hearing your nagging voice! Die already!"

Die for real. Die forever.

She shook the door back and forth, unwilling to approach the old woman. She may be a delusion, but that didn't mean she couldn't possibly hurt Amanda.

Rhoda had hurt her before. But ... wait, that was a long time ago, wasn't it? Right, she was little. Her mother shook her, that was it. Grabbed her and twisted her arm too. She remembered. It was so painful. She cried and screamed but her mother was having a fit over something. Probably drunk at the time. Someone had come to the door. Maybe it was a neighbor, or maybe it was her Aunt Margot. She didn't remember that part of it. But she had to go to the hospital and the doctor put her arm in a sling. That was the last time Rhoda hurt her, wasn't it?

"Mandy! MANDY!" Rhoda's voice was rough and ragged from years of smoking.

Amanda continued to shake the door until she heard sounds coming from downstairs.

Benzos! It had to be them. Nosy Benzos.

She ran down the stairs. The room was empty, but someone was knocking at the front door.

"Who are you?" asked Amanda, clenching her jaw as she opened the door.

On the porch was a tall blonde woman in a charcoal gray pantsuit with a magenta scarf and way too much make-up and jewelry for 10:30 in the morning.

"Are you Amanda Woods?" the woman asked.

"Who are *you*?" repeated Amanda.

"My name is Marcia Silversteen. I'm an attorney. I'm here to help you." She stepped back slightly and Amanda could see she was not alone. With her was Donna and a short Filipino woman.

"I don't need a lawyer," she said, and she started to close the door.

"Please, wait, Amanda," said Silversteen, putting her hand out to stop the door from being slammed in her face. "I'm here about your mother."

Amanda opened the door slightly and looked at the three women more carefully. Donna was dressed the most casually, wearing nice dark jeans, a white blouse, and a lightweight beige blazer. The Filipino woman was wearing a white pantsuit over a shiny teal blouse. They were probably all Benzos. It was hard to get away from them. They were everywhere you went these days. Now they were coming to her door. But she knew Donna, sort of. She opened the door all the way and walked into the living room, the three women following behind her.

When they approached the sitting area, Amanda stopped short.

"So, what about my mother? What do you want with her? She's sick and doesn't see anybody."

Donna was surprised that Amanda, who had only recently admitted that her 'mother' was nothing more than a delusion, was now referring to her as a living human being. She stepped forward, ahead of the attorney and the Filipino woman.

"Amanda, this is Filomena Reyes. She's my boss. I told her about you and your ... mother. She asked Ms. Silversteen to come with us and discuss your mother and your living situation."

"My living situation?" Amanda rolled her eyes.

"Can we sit down?" Donna continued.

Amanda immediately plopped down into the blue club chair and put her distraught feet up on the equally distressed ottoman. Her soles and heels were cracked and blackened, and the ottoman was stained from years of supporting her filthy feet.

Mena and Donna sat on the sofa facing the wall, and Marcia Silversteen pulled a side chair away from its place near a buffet and sat down next to Amanda's chair.

Mena and Donna looked at each other, and Mena leaned forward.

"Ms. Woods," she began. "How is your mother today?"

"Same as usual, I guess. Why?" Amanda didn't like being questioned. She didn't trust these women.

"Do you take care of her?" continued Mena. "Do you feed her, bathe her, give her medicine?"

"No, no, no, and no."

Donna interrupted.

"Amanda, who takes care of your mother?"

"She takes care of herself."

Marcia Silversteen stood up.

"Would it be okay if I could meet your mother?"

"Good luck with that," said Amanda, partly under her breath.

"I can take her upstairs," offered Donna, rising to lead the way.

"Sure, be my guest," said Amanda, with a sneer of irony in her voice muted with a chuckle.

This should be interesting.

Donna and the attorney headed for the short hall and stairway. The steps were narrow and steep, like so many were in old Victorian homes in the area.

"This house smells awful," remarked Marcia as they climbed the stairs. "What is that odor?"

"I don't know. The other day it smelled like nail polish remover. This smells a little like, I don't know, maybe ether?"

"God, I sure hope not!" exclaimed Marcia.

Donna came to the door at the top of the stairs and found it closed. She knocked slightly as she opened it.

"Mrs. Pruitt, it's ... " she stopped short and paused, Marcia right behind her.

"What is it?" asked Marcia, pushing the door open wider.

The two women stood looking into an overly dusty room crowded with old furniture and neatly-stacked boxes, and sheets and other linens carefully folded and neatly piled on top of an old four-poster bed. The same four-poster that the old woman, whoever she was, had been in two days earlier.

"This isn't the right room," said Marcia, turning away to look for the right one.

"No, this is it. I ... don't understand. I was here. I was in this very room. And there was an old woman in that very bed. The place was a mess. Stuff everywhere. And in the middle of it all was the old woman that Amanda said was her mother."

"You must be mistaken. It's probably another room. Come on. Let's try this other door."

Donna was sure it was the right room. The house wasn't so big that she could possibly be confused about the location of a room. Now she was becoming very worried. What had happened to the woman in the bed? And why didn't Amanda say she was gone?

Marcia walked confidently down the hall and opened one door after another, with Donna trailing close behind. Closets, a bathroom, and two bedrooms were empty, didn't even have any furniture in them. Then they reached the last door at the end of the hall and looked inside. It was a large bedroom with old-fashioned furniture, a faded log cabin pattern quilt on the bed, and an overall dingy look that wasn't helped by a light layer of dust. It was otherwise neat as a pin, except for a dozen or so books in piles on a table next to the bed. Marcia looked at some framed photographs on top of a dresser and Donna picked up a few of the books and looked at them. All about physics and the afterlife.

"I buy them at used bookstores." Amanda stood in the doorway. "I guess you didn't find my mother," she said, a slight smirk on her lips. "Didn't you tell her?" she asked Donna. "Didn't you happen to mention that my mother is just one of my delusions?"

"She's not a delusion, Amanda," said Donna. "She's real. I saw her. We both saw her. So did your former case worker, Linda Cicero."

"Oh, I know. Linda could see her too. We both had shared delusions. So do you and I."

"No, Amanda. We most definitely do not have a shared delusion," argued Donna.

Amanda began to feel agitated. She wanted to be alone. She turned and walked down the hall with Donna and Marcia at her ragged heels.

At the bottom of the stairs, Mena intercepted Amanda.

"What happened to the woman who was living here?" asked Mena, looking Amanda straight in the eye.

"She died. She just didn't die the way she was supposed to. She's still in my head."

"No, she's not in your head, Amanda. She's alive. Who is she?" continued Mena.

"You don't listen very well, do you? I told you, she's dead. She's my Rhoda-delusion. A figment of my schizoid brain."

Amanda went to the front door, opened it wide, and motioned for them to leave, and leave they did.

And feel free to take my mother with you.

CHAPTER 19

"Are you sure she's a schizophrenic?" asked Mena after they returned to the office.

"Two expert psychiatric evaluations say she is," said Donna. "But I have my doubts."

"She didn't seem like she was a schizophrenic to me. Someone was in that room since you saw them. Something doesn't sound right to me," said Mena. "Like you, I can't quite put my finger on it. Let's get in touch with one of those experts again."

Donna went to her desk and looked up Dr. Kane's number. He had seen Amanda several years ago, but he seemed to remember her case when Donna called him a week earlier. Shortly after leaving him a message, he called her back.

"No one else was living in the house when I visited," he said. "Her mother had been dead for several years and she was alone. However, she did have a persistent delusion that her mother was still there, talking to her. Typical kind of schizophrenic behavior."

"Did you actually 'tour' the house, see the upstairs, all the rooms?"

"Oh yes, every room, opened every closet door and cabinet and looked inside. Aside from her preoccupation with her mother, she seemed to be capable of taking care of herself for the most part. Her house wasn't spotless by any means, and neither was she. But, she was physically healthy and I didn't believe she was in any danger. Her case worker, a nice older fellow – Keaton – visited her occasionally. Her cousin saw her every week, took her shopping, kept in touch with the case worker. I would talk to the cousin, if she's still around. As I understand it, they were raised together."

The cousin. Maybe she had some answers. Donna shuffled through the file trying to find a phone number for Kimberly Brady. The number was old, but could still be current. She dialed.

"Yes, I see Mandy every Saturday morning at 10 o'clock sharp when I take her to the grocery store, One Life Natural Foods. I also call her about twice a week. She doesn't recognize me when I call, and she's paranoid about people calling her because she can't see them and thinks they're spying on her, altering their voices to sound like people she knows. I finally found a way to get her to talk to me on the phone by doing the opposite. It started as a joke, but I saw a way to connect with her by pretending to be this character she likes on a soap opera. So she thinks she has a relationship with her. Not the actress, but the character. So when I say I'm 'Grace Peterson,' she talks to me. She can actually be quite chatty and normal. Of course, I have to keep up with what's happening on her soap each week," she laughed.

"Does she have a roommate or a tenant living with her? I saw an elderly woman in an upstairs bedroom when I visited."

"That's news to me. Mandy's pretty secretive, but I'm in that house every week and I've never seen or heard anyone, and she's never mentioned a roommate or tenant. But I honestly can't see anyone wanting to live with her, even if it was rent-free. She sees things, hears voices, and she responds to them, usually by yelling. I would think that would be hard to deal with every day. I can't imagine how hard it must be for Mandy."

"Do you know whose voice she hears?" asked Donna, already aware that it was probably Amanda's mother.

"That would be her mother, Rhoda, my Aunt Rhoda," confirmed Kimberly. "I don't like to speak ill of the dead, but

Rhoda was awful. She was an abusive woman to say the least. I never once heard a civil word out of her mouth. My mother talked Mandy into coming here to take care of Rhoda when she got cancer. They hardly knew each other. Mandy grew up with me and my sister Annette in our parents' house in San Francisco from the time she was about 5 years old. Rhoda never called or wrote to Mandy except at Christmas – when she was totally wasted – and she stopped calling at all after a few years."

"Maybe your mother wanted Amanda and Rhoda to reconnect," offered Donna. "Some adults often feel a need to mend a broken parental relationship. Do you know anything about Amanda's father?"

"Harry Crumskey. Never met the man. All I know about him is the story my parents told, that he was a low-level gangster-type, that he committed some crime or other, went to jail while he was awaiting trial, and was killed by an inmate. Rhoda was supposedly crazy about him, and she started drinking hard after that. So, child protective services came and took Mandy and put her with us."

"What about your parents? Are they still living?" Donna wanted to be sure the old woman she saw was not Kimberly's mother. She had heard of some pretty wild things that happened in families within the system. She didn't actually think this was a social security scam or anything, but you never could tell.

"My father died in 1992, heart attack. My mom is alive, lives in Berkeley. My sister Annette lives in Pasadena. Annette and I moved to southern California together a couple years after Rhoda died and it looked like Mandy was going to stay here. We were both divorced at the time and we both ended up getting re-married here. We didn't realize at the time how sick Mandy was. She had seemed fine when she was living in San Francisco. She had a great job and lived in this terrific loft apartment. When she came to Venice to take care of Rhoda, she lost her job in San Francisco. She didn't think she was going to be here for very long, but Rhoda hung in there. So Mandy eventually contacted a friend at Cal Poly and they hired her, but about six months or so after Rhoda died, Mandy got fired. It's really sad. Mandy was always very pretty, super popular, very brainy but a lot of fun to be around. In many ways she was really quite a character. It's so difficult to see her these days, although every now and then I get a little glimpse of how she used to be. It's like the real Mandy is still in there ... somewhere."

"I understand. That's what so many people say. I read in her file that she had been on medications at one time. Is she on any medication now?"

"Not now, but she was. They had her on all kinds of drugs for about four years. None of them stopped the voices. That's the big thing with her, the hallucinations. Or maybe it's only the one she calls the Rhoda-delusion. She's confused too. Her memory is all jumbled up a lot of the time. Anyway, I have never understood why none of the meds worked. She was actually good about taking them and staying on them long enough so that they should have worked, but they never did."

The conversation ended, and Donna leaned back in her chair, pondering what her next step should be. Amanda had insisted that the woman was part of a delusion, and Donna had seen her clear as day. Someone was there who was not a hallucination, and she was going to make sure she wasn't a recurring problem for Amanda. She pulled the file into her lap and looked through it yet again to see if anyone had interviewed the neighbors.

CHAPTER 20

Amanda awoke after passing another day in the tranquility of the moonlit forest and stream. Her head was aching and the house smelled of something she didn't recognize. Another chemical odor, probably from the Benzos. She closed a small window and opened the back door and the front door to let the breezy draft carry the smell away. She grabbed her afghan, and went out onto the front porch. She didn't like to be outside that much anymore, but the smell inside was so sickening. She often wondered if the smells could be her imagination too. It was so hard to say when she walked such a fine line between the real world and the world that was spinning out of control in her head. She sat down in the salty air to clear her mind, if that was at all possible.

There were kids playing on the walk-street, and she recognized two of them who lived directly across from her. They were afraid of her and called her names. Probably heard those same names from their parents. Schizoid. Schizo. Demento. Bird-brain. Witch. Others she didn't even want to think about. Today they weren't interested in her. They kicked a soccer ball around, heading toward the beach, and they faded in the distance until eventually she couldn't see them at all.

What had happened the day before? Something. She struggled to catch up mentally with her life. Then she remembered. Some women had come. Social services. One was a lawyer. Donna came. She didn't bring any fruit. Another woman, smaller, darker. They were looking for her mother. They were crazier than she was. Her mother was long dead.

Don't they keep files on those kinds of things?

At the moment, Amanda was positive that Rhoda was dead. She had her ashes in an urn ... somewhere in the house. She didn't remember going to the memorial service, but her Aunt Margot and her cousins Kim and Annette were there and they said Amanda was there too. Yes, Rhoda was definitely dead. She was definitely a hallucination, the video portion of her Rhoda-delusion.

But that woman, Donna, she didn't believe it was a hallucination. She saw and heard Rhoda too, and even though Amanda explained to her that it was merely a folie à deux, a shared delusion, Donna had high-tailed it out of there. And when she came back with her pals from social services, they didn't think it was a hallucination either. How were these people supposed to help her if they didn't even believe anything she said?

Amanda hated what was going through her mind at times like this. It was more ridiculous than a delusion to think that Rhoda wasn't dead or that, worse yet, she was haunting her from beyond the grave. Amanda kept reminding herself that she was a physicist. Even though the idea of a ghost was more than she could fathom, there was the real possibility that there were logical explanations for hauntings. She had read up on brane world theories about parallel universes and openings – vortices – between those universes. Perhaps the Rhoda from a parallel universe had managed to find a doorway – maybe a wormhole – to an alternate universe where Rhoda was already dead and had taken her place. And perhaps that universe was the one that Amanda was living in at this moment. No, that was the sort of thing that happened on a TV show she used to watch called ... called ... Whatever happened to that show? She couldn't remember. But the parallel universe theory could be real.

Or not.

"Mandy!"

Busy right now ...

The Rhoda-delusion was alive and well and summoning her once again. But Amanda didn't have the energy to respond. She sat watching the morning's last remaining mists being gradually replaced by whispers of sunlight against a vivid blue sky. Aside from her mother's voice, it was blissfully quiet in what was usually a noisy neighborhood. She adjusted the afghan on her shoulders and quickly dozed off.

"Mandy! Maaandy!"

Trying to sleep in peace, Rhoda ...

It was going to be one of those highly delusional days. Amanda released herself from the afghan and got up. She knew that confronting the Rhoda-delusion never made it go away, but she still felt the urge to go upstairs to her mother's room, if for no other reason than to vent her anger at the vision she constantly conjured up in her mind. On the positive side – oh yeah, there was actually a positive side – Rhoda never left her bed – a convenient behavior for a hallucination. At least the woman wasn't following her around from room to room or outside of the house.

"What do you want?" she asked, right hand on her hip, a twisted smile on her lip.

"What were those women doing here?"

"I was just asking myself that same question? And whadya know? I'm asking myself the same question again, only this time I'm talking to my delusion."

"I'm as real as you are, and you know it. They're Benzos, Mandy! They're going to take you over, make you their slave!"

"Yeah, yeah, yeah. I've heard all this before. Now LEAVE ME ALONE!" she screamed.

The room quickly shifted, and Amanda was overcome with nausea. Rhoda Pruitt disappeared, at least for a moment ... or two.

CHAPTER 21

"No, don't know her. Seen her sometimes, walking in the breezeway," said Luke, one of the two tenants in the front cottage east of the Pruitt-Woods house.

"What about your roommate?" asked Donna, standing on the porch, talking to a young surfer-dude named Luke.

"Josh! Come 'ere. Someone's asking about the neighbor."

A tall, sandy-haired man came bounding up onto the porch followed by a lean greyhound.

"This woman from social services wants to know if we know the woman next door, ya know, the schizo. Oh ... sorry," he said, realizing he had been politically incorrect.

"I only met her once," said Josh. "It was about six months ago, right after we moved in. She was nice but she seemed a little out of it."

"Out of it like how?" asked Donna.

"Well ..." he paused and looked down at his dog, who looked up to meet his gaze. "She seemed like she was high, on drugs, sort of sleepy-like, and her eyes were red. Maybe, like, ya know, from pot."

"Have you noticed whether anyone else is living in the house with her? Another woman, much older?"

"Don't think so." Josh looked at Luke, who shrugged his shoulders and shook his head in agreement.

"Did you talk to Larry – Larry Greenbaum? He lives in the cottage behind us." said Luke. "He's lived here a long time and I think he probably knows everyone."

Donna thanked the two men and headed down the breezeway to the back cottage. She had no trouble locating Mr. Greenbaum because she could hear him before she could see him. He was sitting in a chair on his porch strumming a well-worn guitar. He appeared to be 70-ish. His face was heavily lined and covered with crusty blotches and brown spots from years of overexposure to the sun. What was left of his thinning gray hair was tied back in a ponytail. He was an old stereotypical Venice beach bum. She walked towards him and introduced herself, then asked if he was acquainted with Amanda Woods.

"I rent a parking space from her," he responded. "See her once a month when I go pay for it. Nice lady, a little eccentric. But that's Venice, isn't it?" he chuckled.

"I suppose it is," said Donna. "Do you know if she has a tenant or a roommate?"

"No, but I doubt it. She has a female friend who visits on Saturdays. That's the only person I've ever seen there. As I said, she's nice, but I think she might be ... you know ... " and he made a little circle with his finger next to the side of his head. "Talks to herself. I can hear her through her kitchen window. Sometimes she yells and sounds a little angry."

"I hear you've lived here for quite awhile. Did you ever know her mother?"

"Rhoda? That nasty old bird! Yeah, I knew her. I'm sorry when anyone dies, but that woman was bad news. Mean as a snake, especially when she was drunk, which was pretty much all the time, probably until she got diagnosed with cancer. Then it seemed like she sobered up a little. But it was mainly the cancer and not the booze that got her in the end."

Donna thanked Larry Greenbaum and left. Back at the walk-street, she headed for the house directly west of Amanda's. There was no yard, only a bare patio, no porch, and a pair of concrete steps at the front door. No plants, not even a weed in sight. Donna walked up the steps and could hear voices from inside.

She knocked and a heavy-set and overly-tattooed man of about 50 eventually answered. He identified himself as Jason Cooley. His head was shaved and he sported a short goatee.

"I keep to myself. I don't know that freak."

From the scowl on his face, Donna knew Mr. Cooley was not anxious to help.

"Well, you know her well enough to call her a freak. Has she caused you any problems?" asked Donna, trying to appear innocent and ignorant.

"She yells at my wife in the middle of the night. She yells at herself too. We can hear her at all hours. She calls my wife 'Mrs. Benzo' – whatever that means."

Donna stepped back from the door. The odors of nail polish remover and bleach were beginning to overwhelm her, and she suddenly realized what was really going on in that house, and probably in the Pruitt-Woods house too. She thanked him for his time and began to walk back to her car. As she passed the old Victorian, she could hear Amanda yelling. And she could hear a woman's voice yelling too. Loud and clear.

When she returned to the office, she told Mena about her day, leaving out the part about hearing a woman's voice.

"A meth lab? On a walk-street? That seems impossible. Someone should have noticed it a long time ago. Those smells when we were at the house must have been coming from it. Did you call the police?"

"Yes, I just got off the phone with them. They'll be paying a visit there shortly."

"Those chemical vapors could be having a serious effect on Amanda's health," said Mena. "We had a case a few years ago involving a woman who lived downwind of a meth lab for six years and she had a lot of health problems that turned out to be linked to the chemicals she was inhaling. Headaches, dizziness, nausea ... even some neurological and psychological issues that were linked to chemical exposure."

"Poor Amanda. She's been living in that house for twelve years. How long do you suppose that lab has been there? I read that chronic exposure to some of the chemicals used in meth labs can alter brain chemistry and cause extreme psychological disorders. Even at low exposure levels some chemicals can cause paranoia, irritability, hallucinations. Amanda has all of those symptoms. Maybe we're right to think she might not be schizophrenic. And who knows what long-term physical effects she might have too. There could be kidney, liver, heart, or lung damage. Heavy exposure can even lead to cancer. Maybe that's what caused her mother's lung cancer?

"Well, Donna, I think you may be stretching that last theory a little. After all, Rhoda was a heavy smoker and drinker."

"Yes, I suppose you're right. I wonder if Amanda has even an inkling of what's going on. As if she doesn't have enough to deal with," said Donna.

"She seems very high-functioning, so she may know more than we do."

Donna went to her cubicle and laid her head down on the desk. She didn't like withholding information from Mena, but she was starting to question her own sanity. Was she delusional too? Was she so susceptible that her brain manufactured a hallucination like that of her client, Amanda Woods? Or was something else going on, something far more sinister? She had read the case notes again and again, and all they did was raise more questions in her mind about herself. If Rhoda Pruitt was dead, if Donna was not delusional, if there was not a tenant or roommate, then what voice did she hear, and who was the woman she saw in that upstairs bedroom?

The thought was too frightening for her to consider. But she had to. Her goal in life was to help others. To make a difference through her faith in God. If that meant talking to a priest about a possible restless spirit haunting Amanda Woods, she would do it.

CHAPTER 22

Amanda woke with a start. The house was shaking and creaking, much worse than usual. She could hear things banging around outside and in the Benzo house next door. Voices seemed to be everywhere, yelling and barking out orders. She got up from the couch and looked through the window to see police and people wearing respirators and Hazmat gear going in and out of the Benzo house carrying boxes and equipment. She closed the blinds and curtains and turned on the TV, setting the volume loud enough to drown out the noise. The house made a low quivering shake. She sighed and ignored it. Rhoda was angry.

Rhoda was always angry. Amanda came to Los Angeles to take care of the woman because Aunt Margot had guilted her into making this one simple sacrifice that could make Rhoda's last days more comfortable. Now, after practically giving up her life for the woman, Rhoda was still ungrateful. The vile old hag managed to infiltrate Amanda's subconscious and take up residence there, turning Amanda's short visit to Los Angeles into a never-ending nightmare. So far, the nightmare had been going strong for more than twelve years – if she remembered correctly.

Time. There was so little of it in the average human life, and Amanda had spent so much of her own life battling the Rhoda-delusion that was her mother. And even before Rhoda became a hallucination, she was equally as bad. Amanda vaguely remembered the first couple months that she spent in the house. Rhoda was up and around, she had an oxygen tank on wheels, she watched TV 24/7. She had stopped smoking when she went on oxygen and she had already sobered up when she got the cancer diagnosis, but she yelled constantly, complaining, demanding, and never once saying a kind word to the daughter who was waiting on her hand-and-foot.

A month or so later, Rhoda collapsed on the bathroom floor, and from that time on, she took to her bed and stayed there.

Still there. Always there.

It was after Rhoda became bedridden that Amanda was transformed into a private, round-the-clock nurse and gofer. Whatever Rhoda wanted, Rhoda got. Amanda could barely sleep for more than an hour at a time without Rhoda needing or wanting something. This went on for a year. A year of Amanda's life. A year of abuse from a parent who treated her like a slave.

The doctors had originally said that Rhoda would probably die within six to eight months of her diagnosis. They felt she simply wouldn't make it because the cancer had already metastasized. But two years later, Rhoda was still alive when Amanda arrived to take care of her. By that time it was basically a case of having one foot in the grave and the other on the banana peel. Amanda eagerly checked off the days on the calendar, waiting for the ungrateful wretch to go the way of all flesh.

Take a dirt nap and count worms, Rhoda!

Well, surprise, surprise! It took Rhoda a grand total of three years to die. Those doctors couldn't begin to realize how incredibly tenacious Rhoda was, how long and hard she could cling to life, however fine the thread that bound her to a flesh and bone existence. When Rhoda finally, in Shakespeare's words, 'shuffled off this mortal coil,' Amanda was relieved. Well, actually, she was elated. Relieved and elated. But those feelings were short-lived. The Rhoda-delusion came to stay and it didn't change anything in Amanda's life. It was all more of the same. Like a surrealistic soap opera: *As The World Spins Off Its Axis*, produced, written, directed, and starring the once-beautiful but now severely haggard wretch, Amanda Woods, commercial-free, airing daily, on the hour, every hour, from now until the end of time.

She remembered when she first saw the hallucination that came with the Rhoda-delusion. She had ignored the voice calling to her from upstairs and the cane banging on the upstairs floor on the evening of the memorial service. But the following night she was coming out of the bathroom and heading to bed when she heard the voice again.

"Mandy!" yelled Rhoda as she banged her cane on the floor next to the bed.

Amanda was walking past her mother's bedroom, and she stopped and opened the door. She didn't know why. It was simply an impulse. The room was exactly as it had been on the day that Rhoda died. It was severely littered with all the accoutrements of a dying person: bottles of medication on the nightstand, an overflowing laundry bin, a large trash can overrun with medical debris and other discardables, and boxes of adult diapers, one half-open, next to the bed. And in the bed – as unbelievable as anything could possibly be – was the emaciated, gray-haired, jaundiced person of her late mother, Rhoda Pruitt.

"Mandy, Mandy, Mandy," came the words from Rhoda's mouth. "When I call for you, I expect you to come!"

She knew it was a hallucination the minute she saw it, but it was so real. Rhoda was so real. Amanda wondered at the amazing ability of the human brain to present such a wholly authentic phenomena. And it wasn't just some brief glimmer of the past, like a recalled piece of her memory. It didn't gradually fade away or come to an abrupt stop. It continued for several minutes until Amanda closed the door, at which time the voice stopped, at least for that moment. It was the first, but definitely not the last time, that she would hallucinate the voice and image of her dead mother.

The world shook Amanda out of her daydream state. Back to her own delusional world, in which Rhoda was – you guessed it – banging her cane on the floor.

"Go away, Rhoda!" she muttered, clenching her jaw.

The knocking persisted, and then Amanda realized it was not Rhoda after all. Someone was banging on the front door. She didn't like to answer the door. It was usually solicitors. Sometimes the police. All people she didn't want to see. All Benzos.

Never trust a Benzo.

She ignored the sound, and when it finally stopped, she went to the window and looked out. As she expected, a policeman was closing the gate to her front yard and was walking away. When he had disappeared from sight, she opened the front door and found a yellow flyer taped to it, a notice that a meth lab was located in the Benzo house and a recommendation that she evacuate her house until the cleanup was completed.

Meth labs. Yes, she knew something about meth. There was some little tidbit about methamphetamine that she remembered, but it was stored so deep in her brain that she couldn't retrieve it completely. It would come to her ... eventually.

"Mandy!"

Oh, puleeeze!

It was starting again. The house shook and creaked as Rhoda called out to her.

"Go away, Rhoda!"

"You need to go away!" responded Rhoda. "The Benzos are here. Get out of the house, Mandy!" she yelled.

Amanda ignored the Rhoda-delusion. Maybe she could make these unwanted unrealities of her life disappear by sheer will alone. If she had an ounce of strength left in her. Maybe she could control them by ignoring them and refusing to cooperate with them. Or not.

"Mandy! Mandy!"

Not now Rhoda. Not now.

She sank back into the cushions of the couch and gazed up at the moon in the painting. She was overcome with exhaustion, and yet she hadn't exerted herself at all. Her head was buzzing and her ears were ringing, and she was asleep in an instant.

CHAPTER 23

Oh sweet Jesus, please help me in this struggle. I am always Your devoted servant. I want only to do Your will and help this woman, and if necessary, put her mother's dead soul to rest. Please help me to help her.

Trinity Mission was a small Roman Catholic church located a convenient six blocks from Donna's apartment. She and George attended services there every Sunday. In addition, Donna was a member of the Altar Society and took part in some of the church's outreach activities. She also came to light candles and pray. It made her feel much closer to Him when she was in His house.

Churches were such silent and peaceful places when no services were being performed. Not only could she feel closer to God, she could also be uninterrupted in her thoughts. And right now, this minute, she was so confused. She desperately needed to calm down and think straight so that she could deal with this problem that was so far from anything she had been trained to handle. In all her life, in all her years as a social worker, she had never before encountered a ghost. Or, for that matter, anything that could be remotely construed as being ghost-like. And yet, here she was, waiting to talk to Father Elias about a haunting. She wasn't even entirely sure if he was the best person to talk to, but he had a reputation of sorts. And, when she wanted advice and insight, her first instinct was to consult with God or one of his representatives, and in this case, that was Father Elias.

Father Elias had been at Trinity Mission for about twelve years. He was a youthful 45, with a handful of grays creeping into the temples of his dark hair. He was known for being open-minded and accepting, and very down to earth in his approach to counseling. It had given him a considerable standing as a reformer in the local church and surrounding community. He counseled the people that no one else wanted to deal with. He deliberately and diligently sought out homeless people and prostitutes and invited them to attend services. He was openly accepting of gays, lesbians, transgenders, and all other manner of controversial individuals and 'misfits' at his services. And while he didn't make a point of discussing it aloud to the congregation, he was known to approve of birth control and gay marriage. He once said to an outreach group Donna worked with: "It's the 21st century, folks, and it's time for this church and its members to get on board that bandwagon."

She hoped that somewhere within his 21st century beliefs he might have room to shed light on a more ancient and superstitious problem, because she believed Amanda Woods was in far more trouble than anyone had ever or could ever have dreamed.

It was now 10 o'clock in the morning and the last parishioner finally left. Father Elias opened the door to leave the confessional. Donna rose from the kneeler and lifted it back into place, then genuflected quickly in the aisle and walked as fast as she could after him. He exited through a side door that led to the small two-story cottage behind the church that doubled as the office and residence he shared with Father Kovak.

"Father Elias!" she called.

"Mrs. Rodriguez, how are you today?" he asked, stopping long enough for her to catch up to him.

"I need your advice, Father. It's important ... urgent. It's about one of my clients." Donna was panting, partly because she was out of shape, partly because she was so nervous.

Father Elias Antonelli was used to handling urgent problems. His post in West Los Angeles was intended as a learning opportunity for him, although it was actually more of a punishment after the events at St. Lucius. But, he had accepted the post at Trinity with gratitude. He could see that it afforded him opportunities to get his hands dirty working in the community, dealing with the hardest issues that faced people living in big urban areas. It wasn't that he thought these were more important problems than those of faith, but it was hard to make a person embrace God when they didn't see evidence of Him in their daily lives. They wanted to know how God could exist at all and still let them suffer. How could He forget His children?

Elias entered the rectory office and ushered Donna to a chair opposite his desk. He sat down and folded his hands on the blotter.

"What kind of problem can I help you with?" he asked.

"It's complicated. I hardly know where to begin," she said.

"Take your time," he advised. He could never begin to guess what kind of horrible thing might come out of a parishioner's mouth when they came to him for advice, but he was ready for it, no matter what it was. He had heard it all and then some. And he knew Donna and the work she did, so it was easy for him to imagine all kinds of circumstances that might exist for her clients.

After a rambling and almost incoherent retelling of everything she knew about Amanda Woods and her mother, Donna felt unburdened, and a little embarrassed. She felt her body relax and she breathed a sigh of relief at having told someone who was not part of the social services system and who might be open to the possibilities of other forms of life after death.

"So, Father, I don't know if I'm going crazy or if Rhoda Pruitt is a restless spirit – a ghost – or maybe she's a demon or she's possessed ..." As she heard the words bubbling from her mouth, she realized she had officially and fully unraveled.

Elias leaned back in his chair to ponder what he had heard. He had no problem at all believing in ghosts or demons or any kind of evil supernatural entity. Not anymore. The disastrous result of his activities with the supernatural was part and parcel to how he ended up being reassigned from St. Lucius to Trinity.

"Why did you come to me instead of Father Kovak?" he asked, referring to the more experienced and traditional priest with whom he shared duties at Trinity Mission.

"I ... I've heard stories about you. They made me think this sort of thing might be right up your alley, so to speak."

Up his alley. Yes, that was what it was all right. Ghosts and demons. They lived in his alley. And he had been admonished about spending any time in that alley. But his job was to help his parishioners, and it was obvious that this one needed his help.

"I'd like to meet this Amanda Woods," he said, knowing that he could very well be putting his job on the line with the church, although probably not with God. He learned long ago that God was – or should be – in the driver's seat at all times, especially when it came to the bureaucratic politics of the Roman Catholic church.

"How soon can you be ready?" asked Donna.

Elias hesitated only a split-second, then went upstairs and changed into his street clothes. His experience with the mentally ill had taught him that his "uniform," while far less formal than the ankle-length cassocks worn in the pre-Vatican II era, could be off-putting to some of them, and since Amanda Woods was a diagnosed paranoid schizophrenic, he did not want to do anything that might cause her to become any more agitated than she would be under the most normal circumstances. He exchanged his black short-sleeved shirt, clerical collar, and black pants for a more comfortable and approachable ensemble consisting of well-worn jeans, a plain blue T-shirt, his favorite leather jacket, and a pair of comfortable Nikes.

It was Wednesday, so Donna drove them first to Santa Monica where she went to her favorite fruit stall at the Farmer's Market on Arizona Avenue. She bought a large bag of fresh and ripe apricots and picked through the plums until she found four that could possibly ripen in Amanda's lifetime. It had worked before, and she hoped the gift would be another nice peace offering to Amanda. When they arrived in Venice, Donna parked on Little Main and they walked down Paloma Avenue to the Pruitt-Woods house.

CHAPTER 24

Amanda didn't answer the door and Donna's heart sank. Then she remembered the washer and dryer, and she led Father Elias down the breezeway to the back porch. Amanda intercepted them midway.

"Hello Amanda. I brought a friend of mine to meet you, and I stopped on the way to get you some fresh apricots and plums." She handed the bag to Amanda, and the woman's eyes opened wide as she snatched it from Donna's outstretched hand.

"Thank you ... thank you so much!"

Amanda opened the side door to the kitchen and left it wide open, her unspoken invitation to enter.

The kitchen dishes and frozen food boxes were gone from the countertops since Donna's last visit, but the neatly stacked piles of newspapers remained. Amanda stood at the kitchen counter releasing the fruit from the bag and placing it all in a large colander in the sink. She ran water over the precious gems and then plucked one out and quickly ate it, the expression on her face turning from sullen to delight.

"These are delicious," she mumbled as apricot juice dribbled down her chin. She turned and looked at Donna and Father Elias. "I haven't eaten for days," she paused. "So who's your friend?"

"Amanda, this is Elias Antonelli. He loves old houses, and I told him about yours. I was hoping you might like to give him a tour." It was a lie, a white lie, and one that she was pretty sure

Father Elias and God would forgive because it was very necessary.

Amanda responded favorably.

"You can look around," she said idly, shrugging her shoulders and thoroughly intent on slurping up the juice of a second apricot.

Amanda was apparently not in the mood to be a tour guide, but she had given them carte blanche to explore. This was something Donna had wondered about. Most paranoid schizophrenics didn't want their privacy invaded. They tended to be secretive. Also, she felt that the house was always a little too neat and organized for a schizophrenic, at least that was her opinion from her previous experiences with schizophrenic clients. It wasn't neat as a pin by any stretch of the imagination, nor was it clean by any standard. But it lacked the level of disorganization, clutter, and unusual use of space that she had seen in the chaotic homes of schizophrenics.

The old Victorian didn't have lists and photographs tacked to the walls, or writing on the walls themselves. The things found in each room were appropriate to the room. You didn't find, say, a microwave oven in the bedroom, or a collection of garden tools in the upstairs bathroom. Amanda definitely neglected her appearance, but that was not a symptom specifically limited to paranoid schizophrenia. Some people simply didn't take good care of their appearance, and there were other psychiatric disorders that involved self-neglect, such as dementia, brain injuries, even depression, which was a very common cause.

From Donna's perspective, Amanda seemed more like a highly eccentric woman, an oddball at the very least. Not that she was completely well mentally, but if the hallucinations were not part of a delusional belief and were instead the result of a ghostly presence, then schizophrenia might be the wrong diagnosis after all, and eccentricity could very well be the best definition for what ailed Amanda Woods.

"What's that?" asked Elias as they opened a door to a bathroom. A small mirror above the sink was covered by a large photograph of a young woman with long, dark brown, wavy hair, blue eyes, a crystal-clear complexion, and a big smile displaying straight white teeth.

Donna looked at the photograph and could almost see a younger Amanda in the features of the face.

"Maybe she doesn't like looking at her own face," whispered Donna. Then she realized there weren't any other mirrors in the house. Maybe seeing her own face confused Amanda. Or maybe the picture taped to the mirror resembled her when she was younger, when she was happy and healthy. Or maybe, just maybe, Amanda's own face reminded her a little too much of her mother's.

They went upstairs and Donna paused at the door to Rhoda's bedroom.

"This is where I saw her," she explained softly as she opened the bedroom door. The room was as she had last seen it with Marcia Silversteen. "I guess I hoped we would see ... "

"It's okay. Let's take our time and look a little closer," suggested Elias.

They entered the room and at once felt the overly cool temperature that was completely out of place in an upper story room of an uninsulated old house in the middle of summer in southern California, even at chilly Venice Beach. Donna remembered that cold blast all too well.

So did Father Elias.

"Tell me again what you saw here," he said.

Donna repeated her account of the meeting with Rhoda, only this time she was calmer and the story was better organized. Elias walked closer to the boxes on the bed and piled along the only windowed wall. Everything was covered in a thick layer of dust. No one had been living in this room for months. He saw a photograph album sticking up and pulled it from one of the boxes, brushing away a spider that was on it. He began to thumb through it and read the descriptions aloud.

"Amanda's birthday, 3 years old today. Amanda's first Halloween, 3-1/2 years old, my little princess! Bob and me, fifth anniversary party."

"Let me see that," said Donna, reaching for the album. She looked at the last photo caption and then looked closely at the photo. "That's her. I swear it. That's the woman I saw in the bed. She was much older, but that is positively her."

Elias flipped the page but didn't find any more photographs of Rhoda, just more of Amanda up until her fifth birthday party, followed by blank pages. He put the album back in the box and withdrew a bronze urn, reading its inscription aloud: "Rhoda Pruitt, 1937 to 2002." Rhoda's ashes.

A low rumble at their feet made Donna and Elias instantly stop and stand still.

"Stay out of my things!" It was a woman's raspy voice that yelled at them, so loudly that the window beside them vibrated.

Donna and Father Elias spun around in a ragged dance-like duet as the room took on the arrangement and atmosphere that Donna had experienced previously. The bed was no longer piled with boxes. In their place was Rhoda Pruitt, propped up on a stack of pillows and covered with an array of bed linens. The already cold air turned into a blistering chill, and the hum of Rhoda's electric oxygen concentrator began, growing louder by the second.

"Can you see her?" asked Donna, fighting off a wave of nausea.

"Y-yes. Yes, I can see her!" replied Elias. He had felt this kind of evil presence before and he knew it was not a delusion or the product of an overactive imagination. Like Donna, he too felt nauseated for a brief moment.

Elias stared at the vision on the bed. It was not the image of an old woman that Donna had described. The woman in the bed, the woman that he saw – if she could be described as a woman at all – was a thin being with dark yellowish-gray skin, the red and green of her veins prominently visible on every inch of her upper body that was not covered by a pale pink tricot nightgown with lace trimming. Her lips were thin and her nose was overly long and hooked. Her hair was dark brown with broad shocks of silver throughout, and it hung to her shoulders in a combination of oily clumps and grizzled dreadlocks. Her eyes were a glossy black, like the bodies of two black widow spiders, and they stared directly into those of Father Elias.

"Of course you can see me!" came the angry and snide voice of ... Rhoda Pruitt? "You've seen the likes of me before, and a lot more, haven't you, Padre?"

He looked straight back into the eyes of the creature but said nothing. Donna was frozen in place, uncertain what to do or say. Amanda walked nonchalantly into the room, a trace of apricot remnants decorating the edges of her mouth and chin.

"Wondering how I know you're a priest, aren't you? Thought I wouldn't recognize one of your kind without the collar?" said the remnants of Rhoda.

"Another folie à deux," commented Amanda, smirking slightly. "Another person to share in the delusion. What do you think so far? Are you enjoying the circus in my head?"

"Mandy, Mandy, Mandy! You let anyone in the house, don't you?" interrupted the wraith.

"What is it that you want this time?" asked Amanda, her jaw tight as anger pulsed through her body. "Why can't you just die once and for all?"

"You always ask that, but here I am! Now get these strangers out of my house!" she ordered.

"It's *my* house!" snapped Amanda. "I pay the mortgage, I pay the bills, I buy the food. It's all me, mine! You aren't even real!" she yelled, stomping her feet.

"I'm warning you, Mandy, they're Benzos! You want to think they aren't, but they are! They'll take over your body and kill you!" She cackled and the house shook as she pounded her cane on the floor, adding to the creaking sounds the house made as it trembled.

Donna was starting to put two and two together, and so was Elias. But they came up with different totals.

"I think she's the ghost of Rhoda using Amanda's fears to try and manipulate her, to warn her, but why?" whispered Donna to Father Elias. "What does she want her daughter to do?"

"Nothing," he responded. "I think she's a demon using Amanda to keep herself here. She assumes the appearance of Rhoda to provoke Amanda's fears, and that gives her all the negative energy she needs to make her presence known to us."

"You mean, she doesn't want to let go of this life, so she sucks the energy from Amanda to keep herself from moving on?"

"Don't whisper around me!" demanded the spiritual dregs of whatever being called itself Rhoda Pruitt. "I know what you want to do. You want to get rid of me. That didn't work out very well for you before, did it, Padre?"

Father Elias again stood his ground and said nothing to the unearthly being in the bed, even though he was stunned to hear her reference to the fatal exorcism from his past.

"What is she talking about?" asked Donna.

Father Elias ignored her question. "Take Amanda back downstairs. Let me deal with this ... creature."

"Mandy, don't you leave this room! I am your mother! Do as I say!"

"You're a liar and a murderer! I don't have to do anything you say. Why are you still here?" Amanda closed her eyes and held her fists to the sides of her head as she rocked herself.

Donna tried to lead Amanda from the room, but she held fast to the spot.

"I've tried to warn you. The Benzos. They're already inside you."

"Yeah, yeah, yeah. They're trying to control me," said Amanda, continuing to rock back and forth in place. "They're already inside me. Which is it, Rhoda?" asked Amanda, suddenly attentive and marching to the bed. "Are they already in me or are they just trying to get to me? I am so tired of playing this broken record in my head!"

"Donna, please, get Amanda out of here before this escalates further," whispered Father Elias into Donna's ear. "This Rhoda-entity is getting stronger. I can feel it."

Donna began to lead Amanda from the room, this time without a struggle.

"You shouldn't stay alone with her," warned Amanda as Donna urged her towards the door. "You can't trust anything she says," she said, her voice growing louder. She turned her face to look back over her shoulder at Father Elias. "She killed her own baby brother. She killed her first husband too and buried his body between the fence and garage at my grandmother's house. And she lied about my father, saying he abandoned us – abandoned me – and then later I found out he was killed in jail. She killed her third husband too. Buried him under the front porch steps of this house. I don't know what other horrible things she might have done." The words were propelled in rapid-fire bursts from Amanda's mouth, relieving her of secrets she had held for Rhoda for far too many years.

Father Elias ignored the warning. He wasn't sure if Amanda was voicing the truth or the insane ravings of the creature in the bed. He was always the epitome of tranquility during a crisis. It came naturally to him, to be calm, to listen, to assess a situation, to react rationally, even if he was terrified. And he was indeed petrified. But, whatever energy Rhoda needed to keep up her strength, she would not be getting from him. He would not allow himself to fear the restless, ghostly harridan. He wasn't sure of her true nature, but she was a demon of some kind or she was a mentally ill old woman trapped between worlds, unable to move on for reasons known only to her.

"How is it that you know me?" he asked calmly.

"Has it really been that long, Padre?" she said in her rough and strangled voice."You were a part of taking a life all those years ago. You never forget something like that, do you?"

"No, you don't," he replied. "But I didn't take a life. And I'm alive while you are definitely not. Why are you here? What do you hope to achieve by torturing Amanda this way?"

"Not alive? You think I'm not alive? I'm as alive as you are, Padre! We just have a difference of opinion about what being alive means."

"And why do you haunt Amanda?"

"Is that what I'm doing? Haunting her? I like to think I am merely living here as I have done for the past twelve years. Amanda chose to live here. I certainly didn't invite her."

"And yet you taunt her with stories of Benzos. Why don't you tell me exactly what a Benzo is?"

The house shook again and the wooden timbers groaned as Rhoda's shriek of laughter echoed off the walls, out into the hallway, and throughout the entire house, down into the very foundations of the antique structure. Her open mouth was a hideous chamber of decay that propelled its reeking odor at Elias and then hung like vintage road kill in the room. He winced slightly, then stoically ignored the rotten scent that was at the root of the Rhoda-entity's existence.

"Benzos are what got Rhoda. They're trying to get Mandy now if they haven't already got her in their clutches. Soon we'll haunt this place together," she cackled. She paused when Father Elias did not respond. "Benzos! Are you really that stupid? Benzos are carcinogens."

"Go on," said Elias. "Enlighten me."

"Benzoprenes, Benzofluoranthene, even Benzodiazepine. Cancerous things. They're everywhere. They're after everyone, even you. Especially you, right this minute."

Elias stood still and resisted every urge to react to her rantings. What did she really know about him? How could she know anything at all? Was she a conduit for all things that happened here and in the afterworld? And what had she said about being here for twelve years? He'd been in California for twelve years. Was there a connection?

As quickly as she had appeared, her image faded and the room returned to its true appearance. Without energy to feed on she could no longer maintain her stay. The temperature began to rise as Elias turned around and looked at the room. Nothing out of place. The piles of boxes lined the walls under the windows and sat neatly stacked on the bed. Not a sign remained of the viciously insane being that had taken on the severely degraded guise of the late Rhoda Pruitt.

CHAPTER 25

"But she *is* a hallucination. She's part of my Rhoda-delusion. I'm a schizophrenic. That's what I do. I have delusions. Are you trying to tell me that after all these years of living with this hallucination that it's *not* a part of my delusions at all? I may be insane, but I am *not* stupid. There are no such things as ghosts and demons!"

Amanda rose from the sofa and anxiously paced the room. It was too much to process. It was too impossible to believe. Rhoda was a ghost? A demon?

There are no such things as ghosts and demons. Unless ghosts are the manifestations of parallel universes based on the brane world theory ...

She quickly dismissed the thought. She had visited that idea already and decided it was not a viable explanation for the presence of Rhoda. Rhoda was a delusion.

Donna and Father Elias sat quietly, trying to allow Amanda enough time to absorb what they were telling her.

"There's more, Amanda," began Donna.

"Oh great holy hell!" exclaimed Amanda, plopping back down on the sofa and gripping the seat cushions as she rocked herself gently. "What else can there be?"

"Quite a lot, actually," Donna said slowly. "You get phone calls from 'Grace Peterson' a few times a week, don't you?" Amanda said nothing but stopped rocking herself. "That's your cousin Kimberly. She couldn't get you to talk to her on the phone, and what started as a joke turned out to be her only way of checking in on you during the week to be sure you were okay."

"No. No. Grace Peterson is my friend. She's real."

"Yes, she is definitely real. The phone calls are real too. But she's not Grace Peterson. Grace Peterson is a character on a soap opera. The phone calls are from Kimberly pretending to be Grace so that you'll talk to her."

Another impossibility. How could all these things have such seemingly rational explanations? Even though she had always suspected there was something else behind everything she experienced, she was a twice-diagnosed paranoid schizophrenic. So said the experts. Whenever anything seemed unthinkable or improbable in her life, Amanda merely accepted it and chalked it up to schizophrenia. She had built her life around that belief. She lived that belief. And now she was expected to stop living that belief after all these years?

"What else?" she asked, stiffening and bracing herself, waiting for what was to come.

"The Benzos," said Elias.

"What about them?"

"They are partly real," he explained. "They are real chemicals ..."

"I know they're real," said Amanda. "I'm a physicist. I know about chemicals, and when Rhoda was dying she never shut up about them. I studied up on them. Benzoprene and the others. Carcinogens. Rhoda was a chain smoker and died of lung cancer."

"We understand that, Amanda," Donna interjected. "But you have also been exposed to a variety of toxic chemicals over a period of about twelve years. It just happens that their effects on you coincided with the death of your mother and her appearance after that."

"What toxic chemicals are you talking about? I don't go anywhere and I don't use much in the way of cleaning solutions. And I'm not on any medication."

"The people next door," said Donna. "You called them Benzos. And you weren't far off. They ran a meth lab. The police closed it down late yesterday afternoon."

"Rhoda called them Benzos and after awhile, I called them Benzos too. I call anything that's toxic a Benzo. And people can be toxic." She paused and reflected, then continued. "I always suspected that the chemical odors in the house were just more of my delusions. But then I saw the police there. I turned up the TV loud to drown out the noise. They came to my door, but I didn't answer. They left a notice on the door about it."

"You'll have to leave this house, at least for awhile, maybe a very long while. I called Kimberly and she is coming to help you pack up some things. She says you can stay with her until they make sure this house is safe for you."

"How do you know all this? How come you figured this out and no one else ever did?" asked Amanda. "Oh, and those poor cats!" she added, suddenly remembering several stray cats she fed that had died with horrible growths on their bodies.

My poor little Romeo and Juliet!

"I became very curious after I first visited you. I could smell the chemicals all over your house. They probably seeped through the old window casings since the houses on this street are old and so close together and you're directly downwind from them," explained Donna. "You may not have even noticed some of the smells after awhile, even as bad as they were, because you've been exposed to them every day for such a long time. A wide variety of substances that have the potential to harm you, to cause brain damage. Meth labs use very toxic substances. Methanol, bleach, drain cleaners, battery acid, ammonia, lye, trichloroethylene, and others. And benzene. That's not only another one of your Benzos, but it's also a neurotoxin and one of the top three most toxic chemicals according to the EPA."

"It can cause headaches and unconsciousness," added Amanda, staring off into space as she did so. "I know about benzene. It's used for all kinds of things." She abruptly looked up at the painting over the sofa as a sudden realization dawned on her. "Oh no," she moaned, dropping her chin into her hands. "Now I understand about the painting."

"The one where you ... visit?" asked Donna.

"I was unconscious, sometimes for more than a day. I thought the missing time was a delusion too. I thought everything was a delusion, a hallucination."

"Well, I think in this case the painting probably was. I'm guessing that most, if not all, of your delusions were probably chemically induced. We need to get you out of here and get you proper medical attention and a new psych evaluation to see what is going on and what the best course of treatment is."

"What about Rhoda? If she's a ghost or a demon – and I still doubt that very much – how can I come back here if she's still here? Medication won't help that."

"No, it won't," said Elias. "That's where I come in. I'm a priest, Amanda. I'll do everything I can to remove this entity and send it back to where it came from."

"A priest ...?" said Amanda, her brow furrowing.

A knock at the back door broke her train of thought, and signaled the arrival of Kimberly Brady.

"I got here as fast as I could," she said on entering. "Traffic is terrible today and I'm double-parked in the alley." The words tumbled out of her mouth in a combination of speed, worry, fear, and panic.

"We need you to get Amanda packed up as quickly as possible. Take only what is absolutely necessary. There is a possibility that she may not be able to return because the house and its contents are probably contaminated."

Kimberly and Amanda went upstairs together, and Amanda told Kimberly what was going on. It was a rather fantastic story, and so Kim was skeptical, but she wasn't as married to the scientific reasons for the otherwise unexplained things that happened the way 'Amanda the Physicist' was. If there was truly a ghost haunting Amanda, Kim just hoped someone could get rid of it.

Donna and Father Elias waited until the two cousins were out of earshot.

"We need to leave too," said Elias.

The house shook, a slight tremor, and Donna's eyes quickly scanned the room. She had noticed the cracks before, but never attributed them to anything related to a ghostly entity. Old houses settled and developed cracks in their plaster, similar to wrinkles on a human face. And the Victorian had experienced far more than a century of settling, not to mention neglect. There probably wasn't a single element of the entire structure that wasn't in some sorry state of disrepair. She stood up, picked up her purse and briefcase, and headed for the front door with Father Elias as Amanda and Kimberly came downstairs with a single small tote bag.

"Good luck," said Amanda, looking Elias straight in the eye as she handed him the key to the house.

She didn't want to be ungrateful or dismissive of the priest. If he thought he could get rid of Rhoda, he could knock himself out trying. After all, like Donna, he was trying to help, and no harm in that. But Amanda was a die-hard skeptic, and while she welcomed an end to Rhoda, she wasn't entirely convinced that the hallucination part of her Rhoda-delusion was anything other than a hallucination. Even though the Rhoda-delusion never presented itself when she was away from the house, that didn't mean it was something real, however supernatural that reality might be. And Amanda was positive that Rhoda was not a ghost or any other supernatural being.

She didn't believe in the supernatural at all. She was always highly suspicious of people who believed in anything that was 'not of this world.' Even gods, those supernatural beings who were supposedly all-powerful and who had created the earth and everything in it, and blah, blah, blah. Amanda was a scientist, and she had met other physicists who believed in a god, but she didn't. She was an atheist, despite her Aunt Margot's most diligent efforts to mold her into one of those good little God-fearing types like she and the other family members were. In the end, Amanda supported all the moral and ethical lessons, as long as they didn't come with the words 'God said' in front of them.

In her mind, supernatural deities were based on the primitive beliefs of ancient peoples who sought to answer questions about their world, their universe, and found the answers in a fictitious system of gods and devils, angels and demons, heaven and hell. And the modern believers in gods were equally as simple, naive, and uneducated as their ancient counterparts. They preferred to classify the world in polarized terms of black and white, right and wrong, good and bad. It gave them a sense of comfort in being able to carve out a very simple niche in an otherwise extraordinarily complex world. But that niche was so unrealistic. The world was not black and white. On the contrary, there were millions of shades of gray and a never-ending myriad of colors in all things. Decisions were not entirely right or wrong. People were not entirely bad or good.

Even Rhoda. The real Rhoda, not the Rhoda-delusion. Rhoda did bad things, it's true. But was she 100% evil? Amanda didn't know her mother well enough to answer that question, but she was confident that somewhere, probably buried deep inside her, Rhoda had to have at least some small shred left of a good person. Perhaps she was forced by circumstances she didn't or couldn't understand, to do harm to others. Maybe, if someone had seen what was happening with Rhoda when she was a child, if someone had intervened in her life when she first started failing in school and was forced to drop out, she could have been a better person, could have avoided taking lives along the way. But, even with such an intervention, Rhoda would never have been 100% good.

Rhoda could have become a staunch believer or a 'born again' and it wouldn't have stopped her from committing evil acts or erased the many horrible things she had done. She could have believed that her god forgave her, but that wouldn't have meant that her human counterparts did the same. And some of the most horrific crimes in the history of the world were perpetrated – were still being perpetrated – by religious fanatics who committed their heinous acts in the names of the gods of their place and time. History confirmed that.

Amanda reflected on a study that was done in the late 1990s. This was at a time when about 60% of Americans claimed to be affiliated with a religion, a number that had fluctuated over the ensuing 20 years. The study examined the religious affiliations of imprisoned criminals in the United States. The highest number were the Judeo-Christians who accounted for more than 80% of all inmates. The eastern religions combined made up less than a single percent. The atheists? Only one-fifteenth of a percent – at least 40 times lower than would have been expected based on the total known atheists, which was around 12% at that time.

So, as far as Amanda could see, belief in a god didn't automatically install a moral compass in a believer that could guarantee they would not become a criminal. She was thankful that now the most rapidly growing segment of the population consisted of atheists and agnostics. She hoped it would bring some measure of sanity to the world.

Said the poster child for insanity.

What Amanda hated most was that the god-believers started indoctrinating their children into religion from birth. She thought it was twisted and cruel to indoctrinate a child, to take an innocent baby and systematically brainwash it for years on end to believe in a god. She knew there were people who became believers in a god after they were adults, so why not allow a child to choose to believe or not when they reached the age where they could make such a decision? And, instead of teaching them about a supernatural being, how about staying on top of their academic education? Because, when it came to crime, statistics revealed a direct correlation between education, belief in a god, and crime: The better educated the person, the less likely they were to believe in a god or commit a crime. The reverse of this was that the less educated you were, the more likely you were to believe in a god and/or commit a crime.

Oh well, none of that mattered, did it? People were going to think what they wanted, believe what they wanted. Go to school or not. And she knew that many people who believed in a god were perfectly nice people. Father Elias certainly seemed nice enough. He seemed to care, and so did Donna. Maybe their religious beliefs were what drove them to be such do-gooders. And Amanda couldn't fault them for that. She may not think they were thinking coherently with regard to their beliefs in the realm of supernatural beings, but if harboring such beliefs was what they needed to be helpful and productive in the world, who was she to deprive them of their own personal god-delusions? Or, in the case of Rhoda, their belief in a Rhoda-entity?

CHAPTER 26

The sun was down, and Elias sat at his desk, surfing the Internet, trying to decide how to deal with the likes of Amanda's Rhoda-delusion that wasn't a delusion at all. He was, at this point, going outside of the church by not getting another priest involved or asking for permission from the bishop to perform an exorcism or other form of banishment. But he didn't want anyone else harmed if he ventured this far from church doctrine and practices. He didn't want to have another soul on his conscience, and that included Donna's and Amanda's. Amanda was already out of the house, so it would be between him and what he was now referring to as the Rhoda-entity.

The problem he faced was how to get rid of her/it. To know how to do that he had to figure out what she was, her true nature. Was she the ghost of Rhoda, or was she a demon masquerading as Rhoda? Or was she something else entirely? How much did any human really know for certain about supernatural beings?

Elias knew what the Roman Catholic church thought about most things, but he wasn't as sure as they were when it came to these more controversial subjects. So, as he continued to search the Web for information about ghosts and banishings, he began to lean towards the possibility that the apparition he had witnessed was both a demon and a malicious ghost, and that they may be one in the same – a ghost-demon.

The original word was not 'demon,' but the Greek word 'daimon,' later 'daemon' in Latin, and it was eventually anglicized in Middle English to 'demon.' The ancient belief in a daimon referred to divine beings that some cultures believed were similar to lesser gods, protective spirits, etc. They could be good or evil. The ancient Greeks believed that daimons fulfilled many roles, including that of protectors as well as souls of the dead. Eventually, over a very long time, the Christian church classified daimons as demons, who were variously described as agents of Satan, messengers of evil, and the unclean spirits that Jesus cast out of the humans to whom they were attached. And Jesus had cast out a lot of demons. In the New Testament, Luke, Matthew, and Mark wrote of many such instances in which demons were cast out of humans by Jesus. Often, all that was necessary was for Jesus to speak, and the demon would recognize Him as the son of God and be gone. Other times, all that was necessary was a word from Him or, as in Mark 5:8 and Luke 8:29, an order to 'Come out of the man, you unclean spirit!'

Elias noted in his research that many of these people whose demons were called out by Jesus had diseases. And, as far back as the ancient Sumerian culture, diseases were believed to be caused by demons called 'gidim.' Rhoda had cancer. Was there a connection? Did she have a demon attached to her that caused the cancer or was it drawn to her because she had cancer? Did the demon simply linger on after she died? Or was the Rhoda-entity an apparition perhaps more akin to the Jewish 'dybbuk,' the wandering soul or spirit of a deceased person that remained earthbound after death, and attached itself to a living person for a specific purpose.

The word 'dybbuk' meant 'clinging,' and the reason for the dybbuk clinging to a living human could be for either a good or a bad purpose. So, to paraphrase Longfellow: when a dybbuk was good it was very, very good, but when it was bad it was horrid. In Jewish belief, there was no such thing as demonic possession, although there was a belief in demons, called 'sheydim.' Elias consulted the Zohar, a 2nd or 3rd century AD book which described the sheydim as half-human, half-angel beings that danced between the spirit world and the physical world. But according to that definition of sheydim, the Rhoda-entity was not a demon.

A dybbuk, on the other hand, had unfinished business and needed a warm human body to complete whatever that business was. The dybbuk looked for or was drawn to people who were unstable in some way, perhaps suffering from depression or a severe form of mental illness. This could fit with Amanda, and probably Rhoda too, especially if the accusations Amanda made about Rhoda being a murderer were true. A dybbuk might even be drawn to someone who had the same desires to do what the dybbuk was unable to do when it was alive. It would be easy to tell if a person was being influenced by a dybbuk, because the dybbuk would know things the person did not. And the Rhoda-entity knew Elias was a priest, and knew what had happened during the failed and fatal exorcism all those years ago in Pennsylvania.

Elias, working the Catholic exorcism at the time, was doing what priests always did in an exorcism: drive away a demon – and demons were always very bad entities. There was always the real danger of a demon's victim dying during an exorcism. And that was always preying on his mind, because Margaret-Marie McKinney, the subject of the exorcism he performed all those years ago, had died in the process. And what, he now wondered, had become of the demon after that? Had it gone back to its hellish world? Or had it merely moved on to torment some other unsuspecting human prey? Could it have been a dybbuk?

Jewish rabbis performed exorcisms on bad dybbuks. They did so with the help of other people gathered around the person to whom the dybbuk had attached itself. The ritual was different than that of the Catholic Church, but that was because the purpose for it was different too. The rabbi wasn't merely trying to force the dybbuk out. He was trying to break the connection between the person and the dybbuk, to communicate with the dybbuk to find out what it wanted, and to then pray for it and perform a healing ritual for both the person and the dybbuk in order to free the dybbuk from whatever was binding it to the living.

In Elias' mind, the Jewish exorcism was far more reminiscent of some of the ghost hunter shows he'd seen on TV. He had a fleeting thought about contacting the two paranormal investigators he'd seen interviewed on so many of those shows, Craig Merchant, who had his own ghost hunting show, and Michael Grainger, the ghost hunter and author of *Grainger's Guide to Ghost Hunting.* He looked at the clock. Too late! Both men were on the East Coast, and he needed to get moving fast if he was going to rid the world of the Rhoda-entity.

He stared off into space. Elias was a Roman Catholic priest. Period. It was great to try to open his mind to other options, but he worked for the church, and church doctrine said there were no ghosts or spirits of the dead haunting the living. In fact, the only mention of a haunting he could find in the Bible was in Mark 5:1-20, in which demons possessed living men and used them to haunt a cemetery. This was another instance in which Jesus merely ordered the demons to, 'Come out of these men, you impure spirits,' after which He cast the demons into a herd of pigs.

Poor pigs!

That type of haunting would be a job for an exorcist because demons were involved, not ghosts. And the word 'possessed' was the wrong term, because a demon could not possess a person, but could only manipulate that person. He chalked up the use of that word to the variances in Biblical translations.

As for a ghost being a deceased person trapped between worlds, the Bible clearly declared in several of its books that humans were born, died, faced judgment, and then went to heaven or hell. There was no waiting around, no pestering the living. But, a demon could make itself appear as a living or deceased person in order to deceive someone or manipulate that person to evil ends. Could Rhoda have been under the influence of a demon when she allegedly killed her husbands? That would mean she had been under the influence of a demon for an extended period of time. Or, was she merely an insane woman who had returned as a cruel, insane, or vengeful ghost?

No, no, no! Not a ghost.

He leaned back in his chair and tried to pull his thoughts together into a logical premise from which he could make a plan. It didn't matter what Rhoda was or did when she was alive, because when Elias finished reading about ghosts and demons, he realized that the Rhoda-entity wasn't a ghost by Roman Catholic beliefs, and so, by definition and default, she had to be a demon. Or possibly a dybbuk (he wanted to maintain some semblance of an open mind) that was using Rhoda's appearance to influence Amanda. But it wasn't possessing, inhabiting, or in any way manipulating Rhoda's body. That was impossible since Rhoda was long dead and buried. And the apparition he had seen and heard and even spoken to was not anyone's delusion, that was for sure. It was a ghost by most people's standards. But to the Roman Catholic church, it was a demon, and a demon, even one that was unattached and acting on its own, could be banished and vanquished.

And that was exactly what he was going to do.

CHAPTER 27

After they left the house on Paloma early Tuesday afternoon, Donna spent an hour or so talking with Amanda and Kimberly about Rhoda's past, to the extent that Amanda could remember it. She also made phone calls to Dr. Lydia Rolfe, to arrange for a neuro-psychiatric evaluation for Amanda, to be made in the light of her exposure to the chemicals being used in the meth lab next door. She didn't mention the 'ghost' of Rhoda Pruitt, but did tell Dr. Rolfe that it was not a delusion because she had also seen the woman. She would leave the rest to Amanda.

On Wednesday morning, Donna awoke at the crack of dawn. She called in to work saying she would be working from home all day. She was going to solve the mystery of Rhoda's husbands. She called every authority she could find to inquire about the two men. She also talked to Margot Weston about everything that was happening and about the possible murders. While Margot was shocked at the very idea of what her sister Rhoda may have done, especially the murder of her baby brother, she was willing to disclose the location of her mother's house in Oakland where Rhoda had allegedly buried the body of her first husband, Tony Ripetti. Donna also called the police in Oakland and Los Angeles who confirmed that both Tony Ripetti and Ralph Pruitt were still considered missing persons. She also verified that Amanda's father, Harry Crumskey, did not abandon his family. He had died in jail in an altercation started by another prisoner. Rhoda was definitely off the hook for that death.

But Donna was also curious about Rhoda's little brother, Billy. Amanda said Rhoda told her that she killed the toddler. Could or should that death be confirmed as a murder too? She sat at the desk in the second bedroom that doubled as her office and stared out the window. She wondered what Father Elias was doing, if he was really going to banish the ghost of Rhoda. Donna was stuck and didn't know what to do next. She knew she had to do something, but it was all so overwhelming.

I want to put this all to rest, Lord. I want the truth to be known for Amanda's sake and for her family members. They all deserve this. Please, dear God, please help me to make a difference.

In that instant, Donna saw what she had to do. She needed to get on a plane and go to Oakland. Mena would never authorize this kind of action, let alone pay for it. Donna couldn't afford it, but it had to be done. It was the right thing to do. She made a few more phone calls and Delta Airlines delivered her safely to Oakland by 1:30 p.m. Margot Weston was waiting for her at the gate.

"I can't believe how fast you got here," remarked Margot as they walked to her car.

"It was a spur of the moment decision, and one I felt I had to make," replied Donna.

Margot Weston bore a strong familial resemblance to the Rhoda-entity that Donna had seen in the photograph and in the bedroom at Amanda's house. She appeared to be in her mid-70s, was petite with gray hair, and wore a lightweight, pale blue, cashmere sweater over dark designer jeans and heavy strappy sandals with two-inch heels.

They got into Margot's silver 2010 Acura TL and headed to the street where Rhoda grew up and where she allegedly murdered Tony Ripetti. En route, Donna called the homicide detective she had spoken to earlier that morning and let him know they were headed to the Maxwell's former residence. He agreed to meet them there.

The Maxwell's had lived in one of Oakland's oldest neighborhoods, Temescal, named for the creek that ran through it. According to Margot, it had once been a tiny town that was a stop on a railway that ran on Telegraph Avenue from Oakland to Berkeley. All it was to Donna was a part of another big and crowded metropolitan area. They drove north on 880, then east on 580, after which Margot took exits that led them to Telegraph Avenue and ultimately to 44th Street, where the old house was located on the north side of the street between Telegraph and Webster. On the way, Margot pointed out the apartment house a few doors down where Rhoda lived while she was married to Tony Ripetti and later to Harry Crumskey.

"This is it," said Margot, parking on the tree-lined street almost directly in front of the old early 20th century house. "Sure doesn't look like it used to. This neighborhood seems to be on the upswing. My father died in 1974, and my mom stayed in that house until she had a stroke in 1989, and my husband and I moved her to a nursing home. She died a year later."

"That must be the detective," interrupted Donna.

A tall African-American man got out of an unmarked gray sedan. He was about 50 years old and was wearing street clothes with a badge on his belt. He walked up to the two women and introduced himself.

"I'm Detective Johnson," he announced. "You must be ..."

"... I'm Donna Rodriguez, and this is Margot Weston. Her parents were the Maxwells, and they used to live in this house."

"Nice to meet you. Let's see who's home."

They walked up to the front door and Detective Johnson knocked, then rang the bell.

"Yes, can I help you," asked a middle-aged woman who answered the door.

"I'm Detective Johnson, and I'm investigating a missing persons cold case," he explained.

"I'm Jennifer Davis," she responded, a quizzical expression on her face.

"This is Mrs. Rodriguez and Mrs. Weston," gestured Johnson. "Mrs. Weston's family – the Maxwells – lived in this house until the late 1980s. We have reason to believe that a missing man from the early 1950s may be buried on your property between a garage and a fence. Do those structures still exist?"

"Oh no! Really?" Jennifer's eye grew to the size of saucers. "Well, yes, the garage is still here. It's pretty old and we use it for storage. It's kind of a mess back there, but you can check it out if you like."

Jennifer stepped onto her porch and closed the door behind her. She led her three guests down a long driveway to the very end of her property. There stood a small clapboard garage that was so dilapidated that it was leaning slightly away from the fence. The space between the two structures was short, very narrow, and fully overgrown with tall weeds.

"It's a tight squeeze, but it is possible that someone could be buried here," remarked Johnson. "Mrs. Davis, would you allow me to bring a small forensics team out today to excavate in that area?"

"Yes, of course, go right ahead."

Donna and Margot left right after Detective Johnson called for a forensic team. He said it would be about an hour, and while they waited, they walked down to the apartment house Margot had pointed out earlier, the one where Rhoda and Tony Ripetti had lived.

"It was that top left apartment," said Margot, pointing to a window that overlooked the street. "I was only a young teenager when they got married. Rhoda was so awfully young too. She dropped out of school when she was only 14. She was failing. I think she must have been dyslexic, but nobody knew much about those things back then. Anyway, she got this job cleaning rooms at a motel that was around the corner and a few blocks up on Telegraph. There was a big Italian community in this area and one of their clubs held a dance. That's where she met Tony. I heard stories from my Mom that he was violent and no loss when he went missing. But you'd never have known it to look at him. He must have been at least 25, maybe even 30 years old, and he was drop-dead gorgeous with a beautiful smile."

"What happened when he suddenly disappeared"? asked Donna.

"The police were notified and they took a report. That's all I ever heard. It's hard to think that Rhoda could have killed him, but she was a tough little cookie, that's for sure. Whatever she wanted, she pretty much got, one way or the other, whatever it took. So, maybe ..." She shrugged as her voice trailed off. The two women walked in silence for a while, eventually visiting the site of the motel where Rhoda had worked on Telegraph. The motel was long gone, and in its place was a newer, non-descript office building.

When Donna and Margot made their return trip to the former Maxwell home, Jennifer Davis, Detective Johnson, another officer, and a two-man forensic team, headed down the driveway, shovels in hand. The three women all followed the police crew as far as the garage and then waited for them to do their grizzly job.

CHAPTER 28

It was Wednesday, 1:00 p.m., and Father Elias, carrying a small black leather satchel, unlocked the front door to the old dwelling that was the home of Amanda Woods and the predatory being she knew as her Rhoda-delusion. As he entered, he felt a tremor that made the old Victorian's wood frame timbers creak slightly. There was also a tremor that ran through his body, a sign of his own deep fear of what was to come. All he knew was that this time – this time for sure – it wouldn't end the way it did all those years ago for Margaret-Marie McKinney in Pennsylvania. This time it was between him and the demon. Amanda, the demon's victim, was safely tucked away with her devoted cousin Kim.

He walked through the living room and studied everything that might give him an advance clue as to why the Rhoda-demon was there. He came to the painting on the wall above the sofa. It was a beautiful picture of a forest with a half-moon in the sky reflecting off a stream below. In the bottom right-hand corner, in small faded letters, was the artist's signature and date: A. Woods, 2003. Donna hadn't mentioned anything about Amanda having any artistic talents, only that she was a physicist. But whatever her interests, they were not relevant at this moment. He was here to exorcise a demon.

Elias had to keep that uppermost in his mind. To him, the Rhoda-entity was now officially the Rhoda-demon. It was based on what the church taught and therefore it was what he had to believe. He may have been going outside of church doctrine with the uncommon form of exorcism he was about to perform and which he wasn't even sure would work, but he had to maintain the belief that Rhoda was a demon. Donna thought she was a ghost. Amanda thought she was a delusion. But she was real, she was a demon, and a demon could be exorcised, banished, dispelled, vanquished – pick your verb. He was going to do it and today was the day.

The floor boards squeaked as he walked around downstairs and then he took a deep breath as he ascended the stairs. All at once the entire house shook so hard that he nearly fell over. When he regained his balance, he realized that he might be in real physical danger, that he could be injured, and that no one knew he was there, only that he was at some point going to go there to 'take care of Rhoda,' as he promised Amanda. He checked his cell phone: battery full. That was good to know. At least he could call for help if he had to.

At the top of the stairs he saw the closed door to Rhoda's bedroom, but he walked past it and continued to survey the house, looking for insights into Amanda and her mother and what drew the demon to them. He also had to be sure that no one else was in the house. In Amanda's room, he looked through drawers, shelves, and the closet. It wasn't until he knelt down to look under the bed that he felt a loose floor board and easily pried it up. In the small space between the floor and subfloor was a metal box. The lock appeared to have been pried open at some time, but now it wasn't even locked and he opened it to find it packed full of cash. He put the box on the bed and spilled out the cash and did a quick accounting: $65,000, give or take $500. Most of the bills in the bottom were $100s, but the top ones were all $20s. Where did she get all this money?

The house shook once more and Elias heard glass fall to the floor and shatter. It sounded like it came from the kitchen, but he was not going to investigate. He put the money back in the box and carried the box back down the hall to Rhoda's bedroom door. He put it down on the floor and opened his small satchel. He pulled out his white surplice and purple stole and put them on with all due reverence. Then he reached in and removed a small sheaf of folded papers that contained all of the pertinent text he would need from the *Rite of Exorcism* and the *Rituale Romanum*. Unlike his only previous exorcism, he knew he would have to deviate from the text to accommodate a rite in which there was no human being influenced by the free and physically unattached demon. He had made various notes in red throughout to guide him in those changes. He reviewed them quickly and then picked up the satchel and opened the door to Rhoda's foul lair.

Heavenly Father, help me rid the world of this demon. Please, dear God, please show me the way.

The room was the same dusty storage facility it had been when he and Donna entered previously. The bed was piled with neatly folded blankets, boxes were lined up under the windows, and there was no sign of the Rhoda-demon. The house still smelled slightly of the chemicals from the meth lab, and Elias hoped they would not do him any bodily harm. This exorcism was fraught with possible injury, hopefully not death.

The room was cool, but it was a typical chilly and overcast day at Venice Beach. He walked to the foot of the bed and spoke.

"God, who is all-good and all-powerful, please accept this prayer that the wicked demon that dwells in this place be expelled to the Hell from which it came."

The room at once grew cold, and then even colder, until Elias could see his breath hanging like a small white cloud in front of his face. He sprinkled holy water on the bed, and as he did so, low tremors rattled the building, growing stronger until the house gave a great shake and the room began to shift and change. He recognized the wave of queasiness that he had felt when he and Donna were in the room and Rhoda appeared to them.

The room had once again reverted to the sick room of the dying Rhoda Pruitt. And there was the Rhoda-demon in all her hideous glory, propped up on a pile of pillows, her oxygen concentrator humming at an almost deafening level beside the bed, and the cannula lines draped over her ears and coming to rest at the base of her nose with the prongs in the openings of her nostrils.

"Well, well, if it isn't the priest again. Had to come back to see me one more time, Padre?" She made a raspy laugh that ended in a cough.

"Depart, demon," commanded Father Elias. He lifted a crucifix from his satchel and held it in front of him in the face of the Rhoda-demon. "Leave this house and return to the dark world from which you came."

"That's some speech, Padre," replied the Rhoda-demon, nonchalantly. "What's with calling me a demon? Why not 'impious one'? Isn't that the term you used when you were exorcising poor old Margaret-Marie?"

"Don't mock me, you devil!" said Father Elias. "Depart impious one!" he ordered in mocking sarcasm.

" I am no devil!" she shrieked and rasped.

"Be gone from this house and from the lives of those who live here! I command you as a servant of almighty God, his son, Jesus Christ, and the Holy Spirit." As he spoke, Elias sprinkled more holy water on the bed, much of it directly onto the Rhoda-demon.

"You can't order me around. I'm in charge here," she said.

She lunged forward, arms outstretched, and all at once, the papers Elias held in his hand – the papers that included all of the directions for performing the exorcism – instantly burst into flames and fell at his feet in ashes. He jumped back and tried to quickly regain his composure.

"Now why should I leave?" asked the Rhoda-demon. "After all, I live here. This is my home. You are the one who doesn't belong here, Padre. Shouldn't you be trying to exorcise some poor God-fearing person who wants your help? Oh, wait, you already tried that and it didn't work out very well, did it?"

Elias was already frustrated and felt he was failing at his task. He also remembered that an exorcism could take hours, days, or even weeks. A demon could be a very strong entity, and this one certainly did not want to leave, and she did not seem at all phased by his use of the crucifix, the holy water, and the names of his God. He ignored her seeming indifference and continued, improvising from what he remembered of his notes.

"Obey me, dark one! I am a minister of God, and He is stronger than your kind. Leave this material world ..."

"Oh please, Padre, really, this is getting downright ridiculous," rasped the tiny figure who harbored so much evil. "I am not a demon. I am here because this is where I want to be. I am here because I want to atone in some way for the evil I did when I lived, and I want to protect the daughter I never protected in life. That is what you want to hear, isn't it?"

"Of course you're lying," said Elias, looking the she-demon directly in the eye. "It is a demon's job to appear as something other than what it is. You appear as Rhoda Pruitt, but you are nothing more than an agent of Satan himself. Again, dark one, I command you to leave this house and depart this world in the name of Jesus Christ!"

Rhoda did not flinch. The house shook slightly, but she remained silent, save for the loud hum of the oxygen concentrator.

"You will obey me, demon, seducer, liar, and persecutor of the innocent!"

"You will obey ME, *trespasser*! Get out of my house!"

Either the room was becoming absolutely frigid or he was beginning to suffer from hypothermia. The entire house shook violently and he struggled to stay on his feet. She was far more powerful than he had imagined.

"The Lord God my Father will fight you, and he will win!"

"You should do a better job of picking your battles, Padre. You cannot send me to hell. I am Rhoda Pruitt, or perhaps what remains of her. My life was a hell, and I created that hell all by myself."

Elias felt dismal doubts impinging on his ritual. Was this she-demon creating the doubts, or were they coming to the fore because he was failing to exert his influence over her? Or could he be wrong, completely and utterly wrong? Could she be speaking the truth? He remembered Amanda's warning that he shouldn't believe anything the Rhoda-demon said. But maybe she wasn't a demon at all. Maybe she was a dybbuk? Or ... a ghost? And she said she wanted to atone for evil she did when alive. Was she lying, trying to trick him, or was forgiveness the magic word needed to banish her? He couldn't tell, and he prayed that God would show him the way. And, it couldn't hurt to change his tactics when he wasn't even sure what those tactics should be.

"God loves you, Rhoda, if that is indeed your true name. Embrace Christ as your savior. Seek His mercy and beg His forgiveness and He will welcome you into His holy kingdom of Heaven."

"It's far too late for me, Priest. I am doomed to pass my eternity right here. You're wasting your time. Go home to your church and your god. He abandoned me long ago."

"It is never too late, Rhoda. God loves even the worst of sinners. He will never abandon you. It is you who have abandoned God. All He asks is that you believe in Him and show contrition for the wrongs you have done."

Rhoda closed her eyes, and for a moment Elias almost believed that she had died, until he came to his senses and remembered that she was already dead. Her eyes slowly opened as she spoke.

"I have never stopped believing," she said softly. "Never."

She sounded so benign, so human, and Elias wondered if he should believe her and continue. After all, she could be trying to deceive him in order to force him to abandon the exorcism.

"I have done the unforgiveable," she continued. "Do you want me to confess? All right, I'll confess. I confess that I have three times taken the life of another human being. I confess to being a horrible mother to my only child. I confess to being a thief and a liar. I cannot confess anything further because my list of sins is far too long. But I am sorry for all of them, and I wish I could turn back time and do things differently."

"Now make an *Act of Contrition*," said Father Elias, hoping against hope that this would be the final step in releasing the Rhoda-demon from her ties to the physical world.

"Oh my God, I am heartily sorry ..." she began, and when she had stumbled through the entire prayer, Father Elias spoke.

"I absolve you of your sins in the name of the Father, the Son, and the Holy Spirit."

Go in peace now, Rhoda. Go in peace.

The room shook slightly, and then instantly returned to its true state as the final resting place for the ashes of Rhoda Pruitt.

Elias stood silently, reflecting on what had happened. Could he have actually succeeded in banishing a demon? He felt more tremors. Could it have been so easy? The Rhoda-demon appeared to be gone, but the house was moving, and a crack was being etched across the wall above the head of Rhoda's bed. He threw his things into the satchel and went to the bedroom door, grabbed up the metal box of cash, and headed down the stairs. There was a loud cracking and crunching sound, like wood breaking, and he stumbled when he reached the front door and the floor suddenly dropped a few inches beneath him. He ran out into the walk-street in time to look back and watch the old Victorian quickly but gradually collapse into itself and then plunge almost entirely into a giant sink hole, simultaneously taking down the majority of the meth lab house and part of the walk-street with it.

He took out his cell phone and dialed 911.

CHAPTER 29

It was Thursday morning, 9:00 a.m., when Donna arrived at work. She was tired and knew she was in for some heavy-duty explanations about her activities of the previous day. She hoped she could answer for them when she found herself seated across the desk from Filomena Reyes.

"Whatever possessed you to play detective?" asked Mena.

"I know it sounds crazy," replied Donna. "But isn't playing detective a part of what we do? Of who we are? We try to find out as much as we can about the people we help so that we can get them the right help, the right guidance, the right treatment. It felt like the entire case needed to be resolved from start to finish. We dropped the ball with Amanda Woods, or at least some of her case workers did, and that's about the same thing. We need more funding and we need more dedicated people to make regular home visits so that an innocent person doesn't fall through the cracks like Amanda did."

"You're preaching to the choir," said Mena, sighing. "But you took your investigation to the extreme. So, after all of that, what did you discover that actually resolved the Woods case?"

"Well, I'm not sure if it will ever be completely resolved for certain, but I guess we can start with Oakland. The police found the body of Rhoda's first husband, Tony Ripetti, right where Amanda said her mother claimed to have buried him. They're still trying to find relatives for a DNA match, but it's unlikely that it's anyone else buried in that makeshift grave in such an otherwise unlikely final resting place."

"Okay, and what else ...?"

"And, it's probably true that Rhoda murdered her younger brother, Billy Maxwell, but apparently it's very hard to detect a smothering death from such old remains – it's been 70 years. The DA's office isn't interested in footing the bill for an exhumation and autopsy with so little chance of proving it was murder, and since there was never any question about his death being due to natural causes, and since the alleged murderer is long deceased, it's not a cold case that the police are anxious to close like they were with Tony Ripetti."

"What about the body found at the Woods house? I saw it mentioned on the news."

"It was definitely Ralph Pruitt. Dental records were all they needed, and those had already been collected from his dentist back when he first went missing in the 1980s. But his brother was notified and had volunteered his DNA if necessary. They are still combing through the rubble, but so far it does appear that he was buried under the front porch. They think Rhoda was probably able to bury him there without being seen because she did it at night and there were such big shrubs surrounding the front yard of the house that would have blocked the view of that area. The autopsy did reveal that he died from blunt force trauma, hit in the back of the head, and they said a baseball bat was definitely a possible murder weapon, but they have not found a bat in the rubble. At least not yet."

"I also heard something on the radio on my way here about the cause of the sinkhole," said Mena.

"Yes, they announced the cause of the sinkhole. Sinkholes are apparently a common result of meth lab activities. It appears that to produce one pound of meth makes five or more pounds of toxic waste, and that can sit in the soil and groundwater for years. All that dumping of toxic chemicals down the drain can cause the old drains under a house to gradually deteriorate, break, and collapse. The continued flow of water and chemicals down those broken drains went into the ground more in the direction of the Pruitt-Woods house than under the meth lab house itself. It was just a matter of time before one or both of those houses would collapse into the sinkhole that was created in the process. The meth lab had been there for several years, so that's a lot of fluid going underground to damage the pipes and then go on to make such a huge sinkhole."

"One last thing. Did you ever figure out who was living in the house with Amanda?"

"I don't think we'll ever have an answer to that," lied Donna. And she hated to lie, but the ghost of Rhoda Pruitt was something that was far too extraordinary to believe, let alone explain. "Amanda was too incoherent and confused to remember who was in the room, and so she thought it was a delusion. It was probably a homeless person taking advantage of her."

Please, Father, forgive me for lying. My intentions are good.

"I guess we can't have answers for everything," said Mena. "And, Donna ... I'm really glad you took the initiative to follow through. It took guts, and you did the right thing."

Donna was glad to hear those last words. Her words to live by.

"Well, I've got to go now, Mena. I've got to go see Gomez and ... Crandell – both first visits. Then I want to check in on Amanda."

She was grateful that she was able to make a difference in the lives of those she served, but she hoped she didn't run up against any beings from the world of the dead and beyond. But, if she did, she had her faith, the faith that God would give her the strength to deal with it.

Please, God, give that same strength to Father Elias.

CHAPTER 30

On Thursday morning Amanda woke up from a second restful night spent in the guest room at her cousin Kimberly's house in West Los Angeles. She wished she could stay there forever. The bed was so clean and soft. And it was so quiet. And it didn't smell bad at all. She didn't smell bad either, thanks to a lot of pressure from Kim to clean up.

Heaven, I'm in heaven ...

They had left the house on Paloma on Tuesday, and Amanda couldn't believe how much had happened since then. The knowledge about the meth lab exposure made her feel a little bit more sane, and now she wondered how she didn't suspect it. Maybe that was an effect of her brain's exposure to so many toxic chemicals. And while she still felt confused and not completely well physically, she did feel more optimistic, like maybe she could one day be the person she used to be. She had reluctantly allowed Kim to coax her into a spa-like bath, and she had to admit that it felt good to soak in a tub without voices summoning her and interrupting what few moments of peace she ever managed to find.

Bye, Mom!

She had often felt sleep-deprived due to all the Rhoda intrusions on her rest. She had read something about how that could screw up your brain too. And this was the longest she had ever been away from the Rhoda-delusion. The most she had ever been able to achieve before was a couple hours while she went on a walk or went to the store with Kim. Maybe if she could stay away from the house, she would never have to see or hear Rhoda again, especially if Rhoda wasn't a delusion after all.

Goodbye forever!

While Amanda had luxuriated in the bath attempting to feel like the woman she once was, Kim had rummaged through her closet and assembled what she called a "starter wardrobe" for Amanda. They were both about the same size, and Amanda later tried on some of the jeans and blouses that she liked and that made her feel pretty. But Kim wasn't done.

Wednesday was a remarkable day. In the morning, Kim took Amanda to the Fringe Hair Salon in Santa Monica for a haircut, and then took her to a pedicurist who spent an hour getting Amanda's feet into reasonable shape, and adding in broken English that "You need come back soon, and we work more on those heels." Amanda looked down at her feet and barely recognized them. She slipped each foot carefully into an old pair of Kim's sandals that fit her. She would have to start getting her own clothes soon, especially shoes, as those sandals were the only shoes of Kim's that fit her.

This can't be real. I'm starting to feel so normal.

In the early afternoon, Kim took Amanda to see Dr. Rolfe, a psychiatrist, whose team of experts administered a variety of tests before Amanda got to sit down with this doctor she had never seen before. Afterwards, Dr. Rolfe sat down with her and Kim to explain the preliminary findings.

"I can only speculate that the reason you were diagnosed as a paranoid schizophrenic is because of your persistent delusions combined with a high level of functioning. Other than that, I don't see anything that would convince me that you're suffering from schizophrenia. I've ordered an MRI and some other tests. Meanwhile, only time will tell. With the detox treatments for the chemicals you were exposed to, I think you'll soon achieve at least a partial recovery. In other words, you'll probably be as normal as any normal person can hope to be, and we'll evaluate you regularly and often to keep on top of your progress."

Dr. Rolfe additionally prescribed an anti-anxiety medication that she thought might assist Amanda during her recovery and her adjustment to a new life. Amanda, while usually hesitant about taking medications of any kind, felt this one would probably help her immensely, and she insisted that they get the prescription filled right away. After doing so, they headed back to Kim's place where Amanda took her first dose and ate a banana at the kitchen table.

A loud pounding broke the silence, and Amanda stiffened abruptly.

No, oh please, no, not again.

"Relax, Mandy, it's just someone at the front door."

Amanda loosened her tensed muscles and finished her fruit.

That's right. I'm free.

"Hi Amanda," smiled Donna as she entered Kim's cheery little kitchen. "I hear you're doing better."

"Yeah, a little," she replied. "I feel more normal. Of course, the meds help a lot."

Kim offered Donna a seat and some coffee, and the three women sat at the table while Donna updated them on all the events of the previous day.

"I can't believe the house is completely gone." said Amanda. It was almost impossible for her to conceive of the entire house disappearing into the earth. And not because she had any emotional ties to the place, that was for sure. It was just so unexpected.

"Completely. It's a pile of rubble," responded Donna.

Which is what it always was.

"My beautiful Blue Willow dishes are gone," remarked Amanda, her mouth in an exaggerated frown.

"You can always buy more dishes, even more Blue Willow ones, Mandy," consoled Kimberly.

"But where am I going to live now? Am I supposed to stay here with Kim?" she asked Donna.

Oh, please let me stay here! I love it here!

"Probably for the time being, but I'm already looking into finding suitable housing for you. You've been paying insurance on the Paloma house, and that's good, because the benefit paid for that loss will make it easier to find you a good place to live. And, Father Elias gave me this. He found it in the house and knew you would want it."

Donna removed the metal box of cash from an old grocery bag and placed it on the table.

"My savings!" exclaimed Amanda. "I mean, it was Rhoda's, but then I added to it with rent money from the parking place behind the house. I never spent any of it. I can't believe I forgot to bring it with me when we left the house. But I forgot so many things ..."

"Well, I'm sure you'll be able to put it to good use," assured Donna.

"Oh, I will make sure she does that!" laughed Kim, and then updated Donna on Amanda's visit with Dr. Rolfe, while Amanda counted the money in the cash box.

"So my mother really was dead and now she's gone for good. It was the chemical exposure that was making me confused and delusional." said Amanda, closing the lid on the cash box.

"Whatever it was that appeared to be your mother is gone," replied Donna, being somewhat evasive..

Hallelujah!

Donna wasn't sure whether or not she was lying, but since Amanda's hallucinations had stopped after she left the old house, it was probably at least mostly true. Only time would tell.

But Amanda had found a little time to reflect on the Rhoda-delusion, and her thoughts were a little more clear thanks in part to the medication she'd been taking. She didn't feel on edge the way she always had, waiting for Rhoda to call her name. She was well-rested and far more alert. She was sure her memory of the Rhoda-delusion would soon grow to become as clear as crystal in the coming days. And when it did, she would be able to make sense of it. Right now she decided that it was a product of the chemicals combined with her subconscious knowledge of their danger. Therefore, she posited, her Rhoda-delusion was something she fabricated in her brain for the purpose of warning herself about the dangers of the chemicals she was being exposed to.

No more Benzos.

After Donna left, Amanda and Kim headed for One Life Natural Foods on Main Street. Amanda always loved shopping there. She stood in the produce section surveying all the bins. She inhaled the pungent scent of each fresh tomato and handed them one-by-one to Kimberly, who bagged them and put them into the tiny cart. She then went to the fruit section where she repeated the search, this time for the perfect apricot. She didn't rush, but she was exceedingly anxious to go to the store's juice bar for a Coconut Delite.

Life is sweet.

CHAPTER 31

It was late Thursday afternoon. Elias knelt at the prie-dieu in his office. The little cushion on which he knelt was covered with the painstaking crewel stitches his mother formed into flowers and a cross. She had made it for him for his 40th birthday, the year before she passed away due to a stroke. He thought of her every day when he knelt in front of the small and narrow window that overlooked a large bird bath surrounded by a jungle of shrubbery. He often saw blackbirds splashing in the water and occasionally heard a mockingbird's repertoire that included a brilliant imitation of the ring of a cell phone. Today, the sun streamed through the window and he could feel its warm rays washing over him.

He wished he could thoroughly enjoy these blessed moments that nature so often provided, but right now he was far too preoccupied with his thoughts of what had happened with the Rhoda-demon. His mind was a confused and complex maze of questions about mysterious things that he simply could not wrap his mind around. He wanted to make sense of it, but he couldn't come up with viable answers. He prayed that God would help him understand it all.

O heavenly Father, please help me find the answers to these questions that are so troubling to me. Please light my way. Please show me the way.

He reviewed his questions, one at a time.

Question number one: Had he somehow managed to banish a demon? If he had banished or exorcised a demon, it seemed so remarkably easy. A little too easy, perhaps? It was hard for Elias to believe that a demon could suddenly decide to confess its sins and turn to God. And that led to ...

Question number two: Did he send a ghost to its final rest through confession? This process also seemed like it was a little too simple, and it was very much like it was portrayed in TV and movies, where some spiritual person steps in and sends the ghost into the light, after which all is well and everyone lives happily ever after. And so that brought up ...

Question number three: Could the Rhoda-demon or Rhoda-ghost have tricked him? That was the scariest question, because if it was still serving its Satanic master, if it was still operating in the physical world, then it might very well continue to terrorize Amanda – or someone else of its choosing. And this, of course, pointed to ...

Question number four: Why had it chosen Amanda Woods in the first place? The Rhoda-demon had taken on the appearance of the late Rhoda Pruitt and used it to prey on Amanda. Why? What was it about either woman that attracted this demon to them? Maybe the demon had been influencing Rhoda for years, maybe contributing to her bad deeds or even to her illness, and then decided to hang around after her death to torment her daughter. But the demon had been warning Amanda about the 'benzos.' Was it trying to save her or scare her? A ghost could have been trying to save her. A demon, probably not. What did this being get out of that relationship?

The list of questions was endless, as one led to another, forming a seemingly endless string of unsolved mysteries. And he was beginning to think that there were even more questions waiting in the wings that he had yet to conceive of and for which he would probably have no answers either. And then there were the bigger questions. The ones that were always running through his mind about what and how he believed, and how that played into church doctrine. A few of those questions were now coming to the forefront in light of what had happened with the Rhoda-demon.

To confess or not to confess that he had gone against the beliefs of the Catholic Church relative to ghosts and to demons? Had he broken his vow of obedience? And why did he constantly struggle with this particular vow? Should he avoid allowing himself to be exposed to or influenced by non-Roman Catholic beliefs? Give up learning other ideas and philosophies?

Turn off the TV, Elias.

While he had never doubted God, he had so often teetered on the edge as far as his obedience to the Catholic Church was concerned. But he was so curious, he sought knowledge, and most of all, he sought truth. He just wasn't sure that the church was always up to date on what that truth was. In some instances, he wasn't sure they were looking for it at all, instead preferring to stick with what they had believed for centuries, never even attempting to reinterpret those beliefs in light of modern-day scientific knowledge of the ancient world combined with the revelations of the cosmos courtesy of the Hubble telescope.

Elias felt that the events of the previous day had tested his faith and, hopefully, had enabled him to perform a successful exorcism, one that freed a woman from years of torment. Despite the fact that he had not been fully obedient to the church beliefs in performing that exorcism, he felt within him an even greater faith in God and in his ability to do God's will. But he felt more conflicted than ever, not to mention a little guilty, because he could also see how some of what he was taught by the church might be wrong, at least as it pertained to the afterlife. He now believed, beyond a shadow of a doubt, that there were such things as demons and ghosts.

"Of course there are such things as demons and ghosts," came a loud voice from upstairs. Elias recognized it at once.

He trembled as he rose from kneeling at the prie-dieu in his office and stood silently. Was he just tired or did he really hear that voice?

"Yes, you heard me," replied the voice.

The crafty demon was inside his head. At least he hoped the voice he was hearing was inside his head, because the only other alternative was ... No! No, it simply couldn't be that.

Oh, please, dear Lord, anything but that!

He rushed up the short flight of stairs to his small suite of rooms. His blood ran cold and he felt chills from his nose to his toes. His heart was pounding and it felt like his adrenalin was pumping a hundred gallons a minute. He paused in front of the door for a few seconds, trying to regain his composure, then slowly opened it to a familiar rush of cold and fetid air.

There it was in the living area, wearing his old, raggedy, rust-brown bathrobe, and lounging in his favorite blue recliner, holding an old baseball bat in its hand like a cane. It appeared as he had only recently seen it, and it smiled a crooked smile that revealed a row of chipped, black, and rotted teeth.

"Did you miss me, Padre?"

Other Books & eBooks
by Jöelle Steele

Shades

Face To Face: Analysis And Comparison Of Facial Features To Authenticate Identities of People In Photographs

The Small Business Webmaster

A Brief History of the Buzzini, Crosetti, and Martelli Families in Italy and America

Grandma Helny's Old-Fashioned Swede-Finn Recipes

An Illustrated History of the Steele, Furu, and Forström Families in Finland and America

Guía Para Plantscapers: El Mantenimiento de Plantas Interiores

Plantscaper's Guide to Interior Landscape Maintenance

The ABCs of Indoor Dracaenas and Other Related Foliage Plants

The ABCs Of Indoor Ferns

Living & Breathing: How to Make Your Characters Come Alive

Unblocked: How to Expand Your Creativity by Removing & Preventing Creative Blocks

Soils & Nutrients for Indoor Plants

Indoor Watering Techniques

The ABCs Of Indoor Palm Trees

A Tapestry of Eden: A Poetic Memoir of Monterey County

How to Create a Successful Web Site for Your Horticultural Business

Researching and Writing Your Family History

Astrological Prediction Of Earthquakes and Seismic Data Collection

Cooking for Fluffy: Healthy Home-Made Feline Diets

How to Market Your Astrological Services

How to Market Your Small Business

Interior Landscape Dictionary

Anthropometry and the Human Face in Photographs

HR Guide and Policy Manual for Small Businesses

How to Select and Work With An Astrologer

How to Market Your Horticultural Services

How To Start Your Own Interior Landscape Business

Get The Job & Make A Profit

HR Guide and Policy Manual for Horticultural Companies

The Rosary Bed: A Mariah King Mystery

Devil's Garden: A Mariah King Mystery

Under A Weeping Sky

ABOUT THE AUTHOR

Joelle Steele is a writer, artist, and publisher who lives in Washington state.